# Blood & Wine

## by

## Rosellen Price

*1663 Liberty Drive, Suite 200*
*Bloomington, Indiana 47403*
*(800) 839-8640*
*www.AuthorHouse.com*

*This book is a work of fiction. Places, events, and situations in this story are purely fictional and any resemblance to actual persons, living or dead, is coincidental.*

© 2004 Rosellen Price
All Rights Reserved.

*No part of this book may be reproduced, stored in a retrieval system, or transmitted by any means without the written permission of the author.*

*First published by AuthorHouse 12/07/04*

*ISBN: 1-4208-0910-5(sc)*
*ISBN: 1-4208-0911-3 (dj)*

*Library of Congress Control Number: 2004098275*

*Printed in the United States of America*
*Bloomington, Indiana*

*This book is printed on acid-free paper.*

This book is dedicated to my incredible sister, Dawn, who was not only my "editor in chief," but the one person to give me the push I needed.

And to my friend, Sharla, who supported me with enthusiasm from start to finish, spending most of her lunch hours listening to me read to her my latest pages.

And to my fiancé, Farmer, who is the most loving, caring and supportive man on the face of this earth.

# Chapter 1

The cold sinister night was damp with a misting rain. The crackling fire was warm and inviting. My third glass of white wine was starting to take the edge off. As with most evenings, I was curled up in my study reading one of my favorite authors. Topaz and Onyx, my two shih-tzu's were curled around me and each other.

I'm a 37 year old interior designer, I live alone in my big old Victorian that I am continually working on, decorating and redecorating. I read constantly, but only good mysteries, and never go anywhere without a book. It's amazing, really, how much time there is in a day to read. While waiting for lunch to arrive, at the doctor's office, dentist, hairdresser, and sometimes I even have the urge to read while one of my uppity clients is talking to me about decorating in Early American, which is a style I loathe. It's always amazed me that people with the most money have the worst tastes. A prime example of that is the academy awards.

I heard it as I went to close the window. Was it a seagull, or was it a scream? A slight chill went through me, was it the breeze? I went to bed but didn't sleep well, and the next morning I read the news.

An early morning jogger found her on the beach and there wasn't much left of her. The morning paper said authorities weren't sure if it was a man or beast that could have caused so much damage. The paper identified her as Jennifer West, and according to the photograph, she had been beautiful. Apparently, there had been a party at one of the homes down the beach. An acquaintance said Jennifer had left the party for some air, but never returned.

It was a beautiful Saturday morning in September, fresh and crisp after last nights rain. After feeding Topaz and Onyx, I took my coffee and a note pad and walked to my veranda. I had several errands to accomplish today, so I started my list.

When the door bell rang, the dogs, in spite of the fact that they were only half way through their kibbles, sprang to the door yapping loudly. Once I got them calmed down I opened the door to a uniformed policeman.

"Morning miss, I'm sorry to bother you so early, would you mind if I come in and ask you a few questions?"

"Not at all," I replied, noticing how handsome he was, "would you like some coffee officer?"

"No thank you, I won't take much of your time. I was wondering if you noticed anything unusual last night?"

"Well, it's really hard to tell officer, but when I went to close a window last evening I heard an eerie sound, what could have been a seagull or a scream."

"Approximately what time was that, ah, I need your name miss."

I gave him my name, Madeline Fox, and told him it was around 10:00 p.m. as I was getting ready to retire.

He asked if there was anything else I had seen or heard, and when I told him nothing I could remember at the moment, he gave me his card and wrote his home and cell number on the back, and asked me to call if I remembered anything.

David Christensen was his name, Detective, he was cute. Tall, maybe 6'3", black hair, brown eyes and very long eyelashes. He didn't smile, but I could see dimples when he talked. He was a little on the skinny side for my taste, but he was still cute anyway. Oh well, cops are a different breed, they've seen too much and they don't trust anyone. Too bad he's a cop, I thought.

There were the fabric samples to pick up for Mrs. Hawthorne, my dry-cleaning and I needed to go by the market for a few things. I dressed in a cotton sundress done in soft pink with matching sandals with rhinestone buckles and clear acrylic heels. Accessorizing is so very important, not too little and definitely not too much. I added pink ear bobs with tiny stones that dangled and sparkled on my ears. Perfect, I thought. Because of my auburn red hair, pink is one of my best colors. You never know who you'll run into. I sighed as I thought of Detective Christensen again. So serious, I wondered if he ever laughed. At the last minute I decided to tie my shoulder length hair in a fluffy pink ribbon.

After picking up the fabric samples, and my dry-cleaning, I headed to the market making a mental list. Cooking is one of my favorite things to do, my Sister and I hope to publish a cookbook if we ever have time. In the mean time, I continue to create and test recipes.

The cookbook will focus on comfort food. Easy to make recipes, using foods you'll probably already have on hand. These will be delicious meals that look like you've spent hours only you didn't. It's designed to make even the worst cooks turn into stars!

I picked up fresh jumbo shrimp, garlic, green onions, mushrooms and the makings for an alfredo sauce. In the wine aisle I choose a moderately priced Pinot Grigio and headed for the cash register.

Upon my return home, and after a proper greeting of Topaz and Onyx, I spread the fabric samples across my work table and mentally formulated some ideas to present to Mrs. Hawthorne. After three hours of working, I kicked off my sandals, opened the chilled wine and started preparations for dinner. The evening was crisp, and I decided to eat on the veranda. The alfredo sauce turned out perfect, the wine chilled to perfection and the beach was quiet.

After dinner, I took a hot shower, collected the remainder of my wine and glass, and went to the library to read.

# CHAPTER 2

She normally didn't jog this late at night, but she was angry. He stood her up again. This is it, she thought, I have to end it. He'll never leave his wife. Tears flooded her eyes as she slowed to a stop. Hunched over sobbing, she never heard him approach.

"Damn it!", Christensen bellowed as he slammed the file folder down on his desk. "We've got the makings of a serial killer here, and the Mayor will have our asses if we don't come up with a lead soon!"

"Settle down, David", Lutenient Zimpfer said. "We have the same MO as the West case. She's barley recognizable, torn apart. No DNA, he doesn't rape them, just literally tears them apart. As soon as we get an ID on the new Jane Doe, we can compare age, social status, careers, and anything else that could possibly link these two women. We know the West woman was not married, maybe we'll find a connection there also. Does he stalk single women? Does he know them through work, or friends, maybe the Internet? Shit, here comes the Mayor."

"Morning gentlemen", Mayor Martino announced. "Morning Nick," both David and Will said in unison.

"What have you got?" Martino asked. "Not much yet, Nick. We're waiting for lab results to identify the second victim, then we will look for similarities between these two women. Right now we think we might have a serial killer on the loose," said Will.

"Word of this gets out and we'll have a city full of panic, especially among women. Get me something and get it to me fast! There'll need to be a news conference and I won't go in there with nothing! Good day gentlemen."

"Shit", muttered Christensen. "Let's head to the morgue," Will was already out the door.

# Chapter 3

Mrs. Hawthorne was starting to be a royal pain in the ass. Sometimes I wonder why I chose this career, working with uppity bitches that have more money than taste. But, after 15 years at it, I wouldn't know what else to do. So, back for more fabric swatches I headed.

Passing a news stand I saw the headlines, a second victim. Oh, boy, I'll bet Detective Christensen is not a happy camper. Then I read the location which again was not far from my place. It started me thinking about having an alarm system put in.

I stopped by the post office to pick up my mail, and was glad to see the check from the Thornburg account. I hurried over to the bank to deposit it into my savings, which between that and my retirement portfolio, I'm happy to report, is in great shape. But, of course, it helps that my work is highly regarded throughout the community of the wealthy.

By now it was almost lunch time, so I hurried home to fix a salad, decided on pasta and threw shell macaroni into bowling water. With four eyes staring at me, I threw some raw noodles on the floor for Topaz and Onyx, and watched their tales wag happily as they crunched. I decided on chopped black olives, celery, red pepper and the smallest pearl onions fresh from my garden. I rinsed the pasta in cold water and added the chopped vegetables, then tossed it with a small amount of Italian dressing. After placing a nice portion into a bowl, I sliced a fresh roma tomato over the top. I poured a glass of ice cold milk and headed to my work bench. I was excited about my new ideas for Mrs. Hawthorne's bedroom and got down to work.

After a couple of hours of working, I stretched and decided I needed some fresh air. I got the leashes and headed out with my girls jumping happily at the prospect of a walk. The air smelled salty and the breeze was cool as it tossed my hair around. The sun was starting to set as I thought about the murders, and felt an uneasiness again of how close to home they took place. I couldn't help but wonder what the guy's problem with women is. The way he mutilated so violently those two poor women! And how did he catch them so off guard? Was he handsome, did they know him? The beach was deserted at this hour, and I decided it was time to head back.

As I trudged through the warm sand, I reflected about how much I have enjoyed living on the beach. The breeze, the salty air, the cooler temperatures that I love. But now that these poor women are being murdered so close to home, I wondered about things I had never thought of. I made a mental note to call an alarm company first thing tomorrow.

# Chapter 4

Once I got back, I fed my girls and decided to go to "Tony's" for dinner as a treat. The food is wonderful, not to mention that "TONY" is incredibly edible. I dressed carefully, in a green vest that had pasta shell buttons and a red and white checkerboard bottom, with wine bottles and spaghetti on it. I slipped into a red leather short skirt, and red snake skin heels. The restaurant is on the beach, and I decided to walk the short distance, carrying my shoes and enjoying the feeling of the sand between my toes. When I arrived at the restaurant, I brushed the sand from my feet and slipped on my shoes. The air was chilly, but when I opened the door to the restaurant, a familiar blast of warm air that smelled of freshly baked bread and garlic assaulted me. The place was crowded and I saw many familiar faces. Tourist season was really almost over, so most of the patrons were locals. Tony spotted me and waived for me to sit at the end of the bar. He, remembering my favorite label of Pinot Grigio being Santa Margarita, poured me a large glass and served it with a flourish. "Good evening, Ms. Fox!"

"Good evening, Tony. Have you heard about the murders so close to our homes?"

"Oh, my! This is awful, how do we be safe? May I recommend the linguini with clam sauce, Ms. Fox?"

"Yes, Tony, that would be lovely. May I stay here for dinner so that we may talk?"

"Oh, my! Yes! That would be lovely, Chow!"

Off he flew to see that everything was in order, and I sipped my Pinot with loving care. Living on the beach of an ocean, my neighbors are mostly artists, authors, sculptures and any other creative creature. So, needless to say, life is always a party. It's always interesting to people watch, and I was enjoying myself.

Across the room was the local banker, David, who looked just like Michael Douglas. He's really hot, has a million women, so he's not even an option for me. Oh, well. At another table there were a group of men that each owned one of our local art galleries. Word has it they swap wives with each other for a little fun! They were probably drawing names right now! At the bar were a couple of young local guys that started another water sports shop, like we needed another! They were all blond and all tan, and very cute!

The restaurant was warm and cozy with rich woods everywhere. It had a "club" feel and had lots of deep hunter green and burgundy, with touches of oatmeal in the upholstry and thick carpets. Booths were deep and private. Table dining had high back winged chairs with thick cushions. Soft lighting and low playing classical music added to the ambience. Even the chairs at the bar were lush and cozy. No flashing beer signs here. Even sitting at the bar was elegant and trendy.

Tony served my meal personally, not that I was surprised, as I know he is attracted to me. But, I keep my distance. The food was excellent, as always, and I enjoyed watching everyone throughout the course of my meal.

# Chapter 5

By the time I had finished my meal, Tony had slowed down enough to pour us another glass of wine and sit down beside me. We toasted to our health, and I noticed how he watched me over his glass of wine as we drank.

He had those chocolate "milk dud" eyes and I could just drowned in them if I let myself. Along with his muscular body, one that I say has girth, his perfect teeth and hands, (may I say that hands tell you everything about a man), I could have had him for dessert. However, I sipped my wine and made small talk.

Tony was 30 years old, and had inherited the restaurant from his dad who dropped dead from stress and overwork at the age of 52. Tony was killing himself to keep his dad's legacy alive. His mom, of course, ruled the roost. She was in control of the sauces, ordering, badgering the salesmen, hounding the liquor salesmen, and of course, hiring and firing of all personnel. You either loved mama Maria, or you were out the door. Mama Maria was constantly trying to marry off Tony, and especially to me. I guess she figures I would make a nice home for him. Very important to those Italian mothers, you know. Actually, as I thought about it, I'm not sure if Tony even dates anyone. Anyway, I certainly had no intention of getting involved with him, nor did it matter to me if he dated anyone or not.

Tony was looking at me with intent eyes, so I proceeded to ask him if he'd overheard anything that could give any clue to who was murdering these young women.

"Mia, Fox, you know I feel very fond of you, and could not hesitate to keep anything from yourself."

"Tony, you have all kinds of people enter your establishment, not only from our community, but tourists. Can you truly say you have heard nothing that seemed out of context?"

"Mademoiselle Fox, I be so want to spend evening with you, but I can honestly say I hear nothing, I be so busy in restaurant. You know mama!"

Boy, did I, she is like a drill sargent. I felt a little bad for him.

We talked a while longer, but I got really tired of him staring at me so I excused myself and went home!

# Chapter 6

When I got home, Topaz and Onyx were sleeping and barely noticed me. I poured myself a glass of Kahlua, that I make myself, and went to the veranda to listen to the ocean.

My thoughts took me back to the days that I wanted to be a private eye. Oh boy, what a joke, a PI with a degree in period furniture. It sure seemed more exciting than measuring for draperies and carpeting. Oh, yes, and to have a partner like Detective Christensen. Forget it, I'd never be able to keep my hands off of him long enough to solve the crime.

The ocean breeze was cool, salty and wonderful. I inhaled deeply. I can't imagine living anywhere except near the ocean, it's so peaceful. The waves started to lull me to sleep, something I did from time to time, fall asleep on my veranda. It felt so good, so soothing, almost like the warm hands of a lover moving over and over my body. The wine, and the Kahlua, warmed me and made me feel lazy. I was drifting, thinking about Detective Christensens arms around me, whispering to me, his warm body curled around me.

I jerked upright and almost spilled my drink. Serial killers always leave a clue, don't they? Why hadn't I thought of this before? You know, things like locks of hair, fingers, ear lobes, sometimes it's jewelry. The papers hadn't said anything about it, but they probably wouldn't. So far they've not made a connection between the women, or at least hadn't released that information either.

I looked at my watch and decided it was late, and I took my drink and my girls upstairs to take a hot bath. After my bath, I put on my favorite fluffy pajama's and decided I wasn't tired enough to sleep and went back down to my library to read.

After reading a few lines I put the book down. It is so hard to concentrate on anything with a serial killer running around your neighborhood! This had always been such a peaceful island.

I just wish the cops would get their shit together and catch the bastard. For crying out loud, what's the matter with them? This is supposed to be what they know how to do! How many more innocent women will be slaughtered? Oh well, I'm not sitting up all night trying to do their job!

So off I went to bed.

## Chapter 7

At the morgue, Will and David tediously went over the coroners report, comparing it to the report on the West woman. They were still waiting for ID on the second Jane Doe when the Mayor burst into the room.

"Hell, Nick, you look like you're gonna have a heart attack!" said Will.

"The City Council is all over my ass, and you boys know this is an election year!"

"Shit, Nick, we want this guy as bad as you do, but it takes time!" Christensen bellowed. "What the hell do you expect from us?"

"Something more than I currently have, that's for sure!" And with that, out the door he slammed.

"And my dad wanted me to be an accountant, what the hell's wrong with me? What a thankless job!" Christensen grumbled.

"Aw, David, forget Nick, he has his cross to bear too. We need to concentrate on finding similarities between these two women. I feel like we've got the same killer and he has to have left a clue!"

They poured over and over the reports until they were cross eyed. Nothing was popping up as a connection. Totally frustrated, they decided to grab a sandwich and call it a night.

Typically, cops eat lots of junk food, just like nurses, but tonight they decided to hit "Tony's" and have lasagna.

Christensen couldn't help but think how close to Madeline Fox's they were. Fox is right, he thought. Stunning red head, just the type that could take him down. Well, he'd had enough of women in general. His last wife took him to the cleaners so bad he'd vowed to never get involved again. Man, he'd be paying child support for the next 13 years! He needed to keep his zipper closed. What a price. They did it on purpose, he figured. Catch us in their web, drag us down the aisle, pop out a couple of kids and they're set for life! No way, man, he'd had it with women, no matter how hot and sexy they were! Screw it, he thought and ordered a pitcher of beer, and watched the waitress ass as she walked away from the table.

# Chapter 8

He watched her through the darkened night. She was beautiful, but, of course, that's what drove him wild.

He watched her laugh and twirl her hair as she flirted. They're all alike the whores. It never changes. Well, he was out to change things. He'd show them all. Make them sorry for how they'd treated him. He deserved respect. Yes, that's it, respect. But they hadn't shown respect, only ridicule. It drove him mad. But now he was in a position of authority. He'd make them pay, big time.

He chuckled as he thought about how he had the cops baffled. Yeah, he thought, Christensen and Zimpfer, his old pals were so stupid. Maybe he should leave his calling card next time. Maybe he'd try to help the poor bastards out to a couple of clues. Shit, they're stupid!

Mulling ideas over in his mind, he returned to his townhouse and poured himself a large brandy and lit the fire. He needed to give the bastards a clue, since they were running around like school girls. Dumb asses. Obviously, the clue he left with both the prior victims totally eluded the idiots. Did he always have to do all the work?

God, he was hungry. All this made him either horny or hungry. He went to the kitchen in search of something he could throw together. He found ham, cheese, onions, broccoli and green peas, and decided to throw all that together with some penne pasta, along with some garlic bread and a little wine.

He loved that he could rival any chef that wanted to take him on. God, he was so good! No way did those bitches have the right to belittle him. He was invincible. No way would those morons ever catch him either, he could always out smart them.

# Chapter 9

Friday morning it was pouring down rain and chilly. I built a fire in my library, made a pot of coffee and got down to work. I wanted to make a few more sketches for Mrs. Hawthorn's bedroom and master bath.

I put together a few more fabric swatches to show her. Combined with lots of gold, silver and crystal pieces, it would pull together nicely.

I decided to check out a new antique shop that just opened in one of the Victorian mansions near downtown. Needful Treasures, it's called. Very quaint. The sweeping facade was very impressive with all it's gingerbread. And to my delight, painted 5 shades of purple, my favorite color!

You know, my favorite aunt loved purple. She was so cool. I used to spend summers with her and we would have a ball. She was wild and I have always wanted to be just like her. She was also my Godmother, my Antie Buelah. She died earlier this year, and I was devastated.

The good news is her daughter, my cousin Mona, is equally as cool and we have become close since Dad died, just a couple of months before Anite Buelah died. She's very eccentric like me, however, she will not drive on an interstate highway! Not me, man, show me the way for vacationing!

I wandered through the many rooms, enjoying the very beautiful and unique pieces from various periods and parts of the country. I saw a very large crystal chandelier that would be stunning in Mrs. Hawthorn's bath. It looked very old, and had hand blown glass tubular pieces attached to beveled glass rosettes. I made some notes and continued on, wandering throughout the four story mansion. I like to use gold and silver together and found some beautiful candlesticks that would be lovely on the fireplace mantel in her bedroom. Also, some leaded glass decanters that would be handy for bath oils. Heavy glass candle holders and candlesticks for the bathtub's Romantic lighting also caught my eye. I made more notes. There were rich fabrics to choose from for custom ordered draperies. Everything from heavy brocades to the lightest and sheerest of silks. This was going to prove to be a very smart place to shop for my clients!

On the first floor tucked in the back was a charming tea room. I was hungry and when I looked at my watch it was already 12:30. I settled into a cafe table and ordered little cucumber sandwiches and a glass of white wine. After I gave my order to a darling little girl, I pulled out my notes and went over them.

After I left the antique shop I went to the florist. I love flowers and routinely buy them after my flower beds have stopped producing for the season. I chose nine baskets of mums for the kitchen, two dozen white roses for my bedroom and a dozen pumpkins and a couple dozen assorted gourds to adorn my back porch.

After that it was off to the market. I was feeling pretty happy and excited with my ideas for Mrs. Hawthorne, when I bumped into Detective Christensen in the pickle aisle. He said his boss was coming in and would probably want to question me about the case. I gave him my cell phone number while I was eyeing what was in his basket. Budget brand Salisbury steak, hot dogs, beer, chips, frozen cardboard pizza and fudge sickles. Oh man, what a gourmet chef.

"In fact, Miss Fox," he said, "why don't you just come down to the station around ten in the morning?"

"I'd be happy to help in any way I can, Detective." I smiled, hoping for one in return, but didn't get it.

"Say, Detective, I was thinking the other night, don't serial killers usually leave a clue? You know, like they cut off a finger or an ear lobe?" I asked.

"Miss Fox, I'm sure you can understand that if the police had that information, it isn't something we can let leak out. The press is going nuts on this one and every piece of evidence is being carefully guarded," he said.

"Well, of course, Detective, I just thought, you know since this seems to be going on in my neighborhood, that you might fill me in some."

"Nice try, Miss Fox."

I smiled, waved him a good-bye and headed to the cashier.

# Chapter 10

When I got to the police station the next day, Christensen was in rare form. What an ass, cops, did they always have to be ass holes? I only wanted to help, but he had a real bad attitude. Man, if he'd lighten up a little, he just might be fun. Fat chance that will ever happen, the guy had a major chip on his shoulder. Who needs this, I thought!

I think part of the reason I decided not to be a PI was the forensic reports. Ugh, how does anybody examine mutilated bodies like these? These poor women, there just had to be a clue. And isn't it typical that cops want you to spill your guts, but they won't tell us anything. That's just not right!

Suddenly, the door burst open and an angry looking man slammed in. "Christensen, Christensen!" he bellowed.

"Jesus, Joe, what the hell's your problem?"

I hadn't met Commander Fredosa until that moment, and I was not sure I really wanted to meet him then. Man, if I thought Christensen had a bad attitude, Fredosa topped that hands down! Upon some speculation, I decided that going into interior design had been the best decision of all. These guys were way up tight!

It didn't take long to figure out who was the boss here. Joe was about ready to burst with frustration and Christensen's knees looked like they'd buckle.

You know, at this point, all I wanted to do was go home to my fabric swatches and my girls. Some men are so emotional!

"What the hell is going on here, anyway?" screamed Fredosa.

"Joe, just calm down, will ya? I'll explain everything to you."

So, after he calmed down a bit, Christensen introduced me to Mr. Wonderful. Did this guy always look like all the blood vessels in his head were going to explode?

Oh boy, was he hot. And, I don't mean angry, well he was angry, but I mean so sexy I wanted to die on the spot.

He was still trying to calm down some more when he asked me to have a seat and tell him what I knew. At that point I wished I knew more than I did, just to be able to have more time to look at him.

I was surprised that I was attracted to him, I normally like dark good looks and he was blond with blue eyes, but he sure had a great body.

I told him about the sound I heard the night the first victim was killed. He asked specifically where on the beach I lived, he thanked me for coming in, and I got the hell out of there.

When I got home, Mary, my house keeper was just finishing up. Mary was a 50ish, heavy-set woman with gray hair. She came in twice a week, on Tuesday's and Friday's, for the day, and she really did a great job for me. I breathed in the clean sent with a smile. With seventeen rooms and seventy windows, I could use all the help I could get!

I settled in and went over my notes from "Needless Treasurers." I examined the new fabric swatches I'd picked up, compared them with some soft, thick carpet samples, and finally the beautiful wall fabrics I had chosen. There will be beautiful shades of amethyst, soft pinks and buttery yellows and touches of white.

I sat back to reflect on how very lucky I am. I really do love my job, my home and my little girls. I'm happpy with my own company, and never feel lonely or depressed. To think of it, I really am a loner and that's just the way I like it!

I built a huge fire in the kitchen fireplace, and decided to make chocolate mousse, my favorite! I have a huge pantry, and most always have on hand what ever I need for a whim. I gathered my ingredients and proceeded to make my dessert.

By then it was late afternoon, so I poured myself a glass of wine. Now, what to do for dinner, I thought. Ham and bean soup, it will be. My secret ingrediant is Tabasco Sauce! About eight shakes, along with lots of black pepper and onion. Now, a little more wine and I'll make cornbread.

I ate in front of the fire, and finished my meal with the chocolate mousse and decided to take a long hot bath.

The bathtub sat in the middle of the room surrounded by beautiful cabinetry. Highly polished black marble covered the floor and the room had a Roman influence. There was a curved wall of leaded glass with a long arched window seat covered with gold satin cusions. Decanters of bath oils and gold and onyx candlesticks surrounded the tub on the ample top surfaces of the cabinet, along with a basket of thick white bath sheets. What seemed like miles of countertops were also marble, only in white, that made a striking contrast to the floor. The sink was a large white glass bowl with a gold plated swan, wings spread, arched over the bowl in anticipation of providing water to its master. There was a separate area for the hugh shower with 15 water blasting heads coming from all directions. Heavy white fabric with gold braid trim and tassles gave the shower area a definite Roman statement. A large linen closet was cleaverly hidden behind double beveled full length mirrors.

I relaxed in the large tub with water jetting from all directions at me. After the day I had at the police station, I needed it! The girls were running around the tub at top speed, and having a ball. Finally they settled down, so I added more hot water and lit the candles. A special dimming switch was installed within reach, so I dimmed the lights and sunk down into the tub letting the tension flow from my body.

# Chapter 11

It was a beautiful, crisp Saturday morning, and I decided I needed a female infusion in my life after Christensen and Fredosa. I headed my silver BMW convertible towards the Mountains to see the only person in my life that understood and accepted me with all my flaws, my sister, Dawn.

She is a park ranger, and a damn good one. She's received many awards and medals for all her heroic work. She's so exceptional. Looks like Victoria Principal, and is as smart as hell. She never really had to study, she was just always smart.

Me, hell, I needed to study, but I thought I'd just get married and have a family and be happy. So, consequently, I was a c+ student and really didn't care. Who gave a shit about history or biology, unless you were going into that field? It really drove me crazy, but, you know, in the 70's nobody asked. They just crammed it down your throat. These losers today, what are they, gen x'ers, y-something. Whatever. I definitely needed a break.

I called Dawn on my cell phone, and when she answered she was busy feeding a baby raccoon that had been abandoned by its mother. I could hear the suckling sounds it made on the baby bottle, and had to smile to myself. If there was anywhere to go to get in touch with reality it was my sister Dawn's.

You know, it's not always that we got along. I remember locking her in the closet of our bedroom and screaming, spiders, spiders! That's when Dad made sure that the closet door never shut tight again. She's always held that against me, but I love her still. Sisters are special. I can't imagine being on this earth without her. She is incredible.

I arrived around 4:30, and true to form, she had a large glass of chilled wine poured for me. We toasted, mine white, hers red, to life. She also had prepared chilled shrimp, caviar, herring, and many other delicacies to feast upon.

As we caught up on each others adventures, we took our cocktails out on the deck where a storm was brewing. I was breathing in the cool mountain air, enjoying the view, which included pine trees, a creek and mountains, when I thought I saw a figure duck behind a rock. No way, I thought. I've just had too much of Christensen and Fredosa! Men! They'll make you crazy!

## Chapter 12

Dawn has an amazing man, Wayne, who is the greatest man God ever put on this crummy ass earth. He is so special. When Wayne arrived, I gave him the kind of hug and kiss that would make Dawn crazy, and we all settled in.

I really wanted to talk about the murders, but Wayne brought in hot Chinese food and we all settled before the blazing fire in the big stone fireplace and enjoyed our Chinese meal.

I was really tired from the week I had, and I wanted to give Dawn and Wayne some time together, so I thanked Wayne for dinner, gathered my girls and my latest mystery novel and went to the guest bedroom.

Up until now I had been attracted to Detective Christensen, however, upon the arrival of Commander Fredosa I was surprised that I even thought he was good looking. I'm usually attracted to the tall, dark and handsome. Joe Fredosa was probably 5' 10", light brown, almost blond hair and the bluest eyes I've ever seen. But those eyes held so much history, he'd seen so much already in his life, looking into them was almost overwhelming. But his hands, they were incredible. I just wanted to touch them, they were so perfect. You know, as I thought about him, almost everything about him was perfect.

That was scary. Man, what was wrong with me? I hadn't had a date in nine years, and I wasn't ever going to get involved again, especially with a cop! I had resigned myself to that much. Maybe I just needed a vacation. I made a mental note to call my single friend Carla when I got home, to plan a little get away.

The next morning, I remarked that the sight of the sun rising over the mountains is enough to make anyone forget about their problems. Dawn and I sat on the deck while Topaz, Onyx, and her babies, Denver and Dakota wandered around the back yard. We love our Shih-tzu's, they're the best companions. They love you no matter what stupid things you do or say. Unconditional love is hard to find. We were munching on fruit and almonds, and after Dawn had filled me in on the latest of abandoned critters, she informed me she had been concerned about the murders over in my neck of the woods. I filled her in on what I knew and my experience with Christensen and Fredosa. We then decided that it was time to go shopping.

After a lovely day of spending money and having lunch at a trendy, popular restaurant, we went back to her house and our girls. Dawn's home is so earthy, kind of like a log cabin, but classier. She is an exceptional landscaper, and her home was one you just immediately felt comfortable in. We fed the babies, opened a chilled bottle of Chardonnay and built a fire. She decided to prepare her favorite "Penny Buns" and I went to work on a lobster salad.

We had a lovely evening, as we always do, remembering funny things from our past and our childhood, and remembering people from our past too.

We sat in front of the blazing fire and just enjoyed each others company. We really have become the best of friends in our adult life, and that really is incredible, because we are totally opposites in every sense of the word. She truly is my best friend.

We laughed over stories of old boyfriends, about how I used to sneak out of the house when Mom and Dad didn't know it, and all the kinds of trouble I seemed to always get myself in. She never did anything wrong! Just me, the dare devil.

We decided it was time to call it a night and headed to our bedrooms. I felt so good, so relaxed here with her. It definitely was just what the doctor ordered.

The next morning, we had a breakfast of grapefruit, chilled orange juice, toast and coffee in the gazebo. It was cool, clear and beautiful.

For the major part of the day, we wandered around the little town, in and out of small boutiques, quaint little shops and antique stores. We lunched on crunchy crab cakes, coleslaw and beer.

By the time we got home late that afternoon laden with our purchases, Wayne was there doing chores.

Dawn always had a collection of racoons, chickens, and what ever else came along.

Wayne grilled steaks, I whipped up a fresh salad, Dawn made garlicky french bread, and, of course, their must be a potato involved for Wayne! So we threw three potatoes into the oven.

We were all such good friends, and we had a wonderful evening.

# Chapter 13

As I drove home on Monday morning, I had to wonder if maybe I might be ready for a relationship again. OK, maybe a relationship, but never, never was a man living with me again, or was I getting married. You know, it would really be nice to have a man take me out to dinner. Stop it, I thought! This is ridiculous, as soon as I get home I'll call Carla and we'll plan a trip.

The drive home was pretty uneventful and when I pulled into my driveway Mr. UPS was just setting a box on my porch. You know, I once heard that the men that got laid the most were the UPS delivery guys. More than cops, fireman and military men! Whatever, nice brown uniform Mr. UPS. I politely thanked him and hurried inside hoping these were my new accessories for Mrs. Hawthorns bedroom I had ordered from one of my favorite suppliers.

As I entered my house, my phone was ringing incessantly. I grabbed it just before the recorder picked up and to my surprise it was Commander Fredosa. He informed me that after his discussion of the case with Detective Christensen, he needed to talk to me again. I suggested we meet at Tony's for a cocktail and he agreed.

O.K., what to wear? I ran to the closet and was clueless as to what to do. I remember once Dawn suggested I put all this on my computer with ideas for matching accessories and mix and match ideas, and I had laughed at her! At that moment I would have given anything to have taken her seriously. I love to shop and I buy fun clothes. I used to be into the tailored look, all prim and proper, but not anymore. I love the fun, resort, and creative look. I decided on a soft, long flowing heavy cotton dress with a matching shawl, as it would be cool on the beach and I wanted to walk. The color was a rich coral, so I slipped into matching strappy sandals, snapped on some snazzy ear bobs and headed out the door.

The evening was cool, but not cold and I felt exhilarated. When I walked into Tony's and saw Joe, my breath caught in my throat. He had on tight black jeans, a black police tee shirt and leather jacket. Holy shit, I knew right then and there I was in big trouble. He hadn't noticed me come in yet and was talking on his cell phone which allowed me more time to look him over. He just radiated sex and probably didn't even know it! He looked a little agitated, but not nearly as much as the other afternoon. His blue eyes flashing, he was pacing back and forth in front of the booth, and I noticed a nearly full beer bottle on the table. Suddenly he snapped the phone shut and looked directly at me. I immediately had the feeling that nothing escaped him, and I only thought he didn't see me come in. As I headed to the booth I felt his eyes give me the once over. I felt a little heat on my cheeks, but smiled brightly as I approached. He thanked me for coming and the waiter appeared. "Ah, Ms. Fox, will it be your usual?" "Yes, Antonio, that will be fine, thank you."

"You come here often?" Joe asked.

"Well, it's close to home for me, and sometimes I treat myself to dinner out. I really love to cook, but, I also love to socialize." At that moment I thought of my favorite friend Carla. That was her specialty, socializing.

Antonio arrived just then with my Pinot and we got down to business. I might add at this point that it is very hard to get down to business with Commander Joe Fredosa because of this magnetic attraction he has! My thoughts were so X-rated! He has the sweetest lips and some, almost dimples, a cute little nose, perfect ears and that military cut hair. But, I think the things that make me the most crazy are his eyes, mouth and hands. Not to mention his body! I would guess him to be 5' 10" 200 pounds. His whole body looked muscular. I like to call it "girth". And boy, was I imagining what else had girth! Stop it!, I chastised myself. What was wrong with me?

At this point he was looking at me with a smirk. I was mortified! Could he tell what I was thinking? I didn't know what to do so I took a delicate sip of my wine and tried to ignore him.

Commander Fredosa couldn't help but notice her flushed cheeks and bright eyes when she entered the restaurant. God, was she stunning. If he wasn't careful, he could fall for a babe like her. Jesus, what a body! The damned dress she was wearing clung to her curves, and oh, they were nice, he thought.

Just then he asked me if I had had dinner, and I said that I hadn't taken the time. He then proceeded to ask if I'd like to, and I responded with what I'd hoped would sound nonchalant either way.

"What would you recommend," he asked.

"The Garlic Shrimp Alfredo, prepared with green onions and mushrooms."

"Sounds good to me," he said and motioned for Antonio, and ordered for both of us. I certainly hoped at this point that I did not look impressed. I really just love it when a man orders. He also ordered a bottle of the Pinot I was drinking. Oh, brother, this is not good. But, it turned out to be a wonderful evening.

He asked if he could walk me to my car or give me a ride. I told him that I walked because it was close. When he offered a ride again, I accepted. When we pulled up to my house, I asked him in for a night cap, and he accepted.

# Chapter 14

I'm going to tell you right now that I knew this was dangerous, but I couldn't stop myself. The wine made me feel warm and soft, he made me feel sexy. This is not a good combination. He built a fire in the kitchen fireplace and I poured my homemade Kahlua over ice and added a splash of cream. We settled into my Queen Ann chairs with our drinks and it felt so comfortable being with him.

My kitchen is a true gathering place. Gourmet pots and pans, and mesh bags of garlic hang from a grape ensconced pot rack over a huge center island. This is where I love to work with my vegetables, and have a tiny sink in the island just for that. Highly polished rose colored marble coveres the floor. Cinnamon Spice DuPont Zodiaq Quartz richly covers the counter surfaces. On one entire long wall, floor to ceiling, were custom built wine and champagne racks done in a rich mahogany wood. I have some very old exquisite wines and champagnes in vintage boxes, as well as trendy Italian wines. I don't like California wines, because they are too sweet for my taste. However, I do keep on hand some lighter, less dry wines and sweeter Martini & Rossi Asti's for my guests. The cabinets were custom designed, also in the rich mahogany, some with glass doors lit with tiny accent bulbs that shown down on the beautiful pieces displayed. Recessed under cabinet lighting played softly on the beautiful counters. The huge fireplace was stone, and the mantle was, again, mohogony, and heavy Italian candlesticks on pedistals with rose colored marble were scattered about, along with family snapshots framed in unique and interesting frames. There were also small crystal candle cups flickering happily. There were two Queen Anne chairs that flanked the fire place, covered in a rich brocade wine bottle design. Between the chairs, a charming scalloped table made of heavy oak with curvy legs and a tiny shelf under the heavy top, that my Dad made for my Mom when they were first married. Under it was a thick antique rug that picked up the beautiful rose and cinnamon of the marble floors and counters, and was fringed in a soft fluffy cream fringe. The kitchen was huge and truly a gourmet's delight. There were very deep sinks, made for the hugh pots used for pasta's. The range was Jen Air, and the large refrigerator/freezer was Sub Zero. On another wall, two built in ovens with a warming oven underneath.

We had several things in common, jazz clubs, antique shopping and we liked the same movies. When I got up to refill our glasses he also got up and came to stand beside me. I knew he wanted to kiss me, and just as he leaned over to do so, his cell phone rang. He muttered something under his breath and flipped it open. He listened all of five seconds then gruffly said, "I'll be right there".

"There's another one, isn't there?" I asked. "Yup" was all he said and headed for the door. He looked back at me once, and then he was gone.

She was only a mile down the beach and when he arrived Christensen was already there, and the CS techs had already roped off the beach with yellow tape.

The first mission of a crime scene officer is controlling the scene so that contamination remains minimal and evidence doesn't vanish. This can happen by accident or at the hands of souvenir hunters, or the perp himself masquerading as a bystander. Christensen had on new crime scene overalls, a hooded full body-suit made of white Tyvek. This prevents the searcher from sloughing off his own trace evidence, or DNA, and contaminating the scene.

Christensen had already begun walking the grid. The phrase describes one of the techniques for physically searching a crime scene for clues. The CS officer walks the floor or ground in one direction, back and forth, then turns perpendicular and covers the same ground again. The theory being is that you can see things from one angle that you might miss from another.

Joe watched another CS tech bring in the VMD. Vacuum metal deposition is considered the Rolls-Royce of fingerprint raising devices. It involves binding a microscopic coating of metal to an object and then radiating it.

Oh, boy, Christensen was bagging something! Finally, a break, Joe thought.

# Chapter 15

This felt so good, success is wonderful. He really almost laughed his ass off. Those sissies are running around with their panties in a wad!

He decided it was a night for celebration, and opened a bottle of Perrier Jouet. He loved classical music and put on the latest CD from Sarah Brightman. It made him feel like he was at Mass. Just like when he was an alter boy. What a joke, wearing those long dress things! God, he was mortified! But, you know, mother had to be a big wig in the Catholic church. Everyone thought she was a saint. Went to mass every morning, played the organ since she was thirteen years old, then came home and got drunk and beat him up. He hated it, and he hated her. It's no wonder he had never been successful with women, she had suffocated him. Always squeezing him against her after she had belittled him, told him how ugly he was and knocked him around, night after night. And now, women just knew he was different, weird. What ever, he would show them! He was showing them!

He turned the music up loud. Screw his neighbors, bunch of liberals that they were. He needed to celebrate! And, that's exactly what he was going to do.

He decided it was time to try a new recipe he'd created. Turkey, dressing and dried cranberries. It needed about 4-5 hours to bake, but that would give him plenty of time to get drunk. Tomorrow was Saturday and he could sleep in.

He put his dinner in the oven, sipped the Pierrier Jouet, enjoying the bubbles, the lightness and how it made him feel. Life is good, he thought, as he stretched out on the recliner on his deck, overlooking the ocean. The cool breeze ruffled his hair, and he thought of Madeline Fox just down the beach and wondered what she was doing right now.

# Chapter 16

As Christensen headed to the squad car, Fredosa approached, asking "What have you got, David?"

"Don't know, Joe. Let's get to the lab and see what this means."

"Jesus, David, is this the first lead we have?"

"Seems like it, Joe. Sucks, doesn't it?"

"The big one!", Joe exclaimed.

They rode in silence, both hoping this would be their first break. Christensen had bagged tissue around a laceration he found on the vic's skull. Silently he wondered if the other two victims had the same laceration, by chance. On the latest vic, her hair had been tangled near the wound. It just seemed different than the other damage. Like a straight cut, unlike the torn wounds over the rest of the body. If the wound was caused by a knife, or a blade of some sort, the VMD might raise a print from the trace evidence.

At the lab the pathologist went to work. Joe suggested they grab some coffee from the machine. After his dinner with Madeline and all the alcohol he'd consumed, he wanted to clear his head. The coffee was like crank case oil as always, but he needed the caffeine to clear the wooziness.

As they silently sipped their coffee, Joe's mind wandered back to Madeline. Her hair was thick and full and soft with its natural curl. He'd noticed that depending on her mood the color of her eyes changed. If she was mellow, they were blue. If she was excited or angry, they were green. Otherwise they were a soft gray. Her smile, ah yes, her pillow lips and perfect teeth made him want to kiss her. He had almost done so before the call from Christensen interrupted them. She acted like she wanted him to kiss her. She leaned toward him, before the damn cell phone rang. God only knows what might have happened. He definitely wanted to do more than kiss her. Her skin was flawless and her figure was totally woman. These girls that think skinny is sexy. No way, men liked women that had some meat to their figure. Not somebody that would poke them to death with their bones! The way she dressed was guaranteed to make his blood pressure boil. The dress she had on toninght draped like liquid over the tight high curves of her butt and ample bust. Her make-up was always subtle, but not so subtle it failed to outline the lush fullness of her mouth, the cutting blades of her cheekbones, or her dark, groomed eyebrows, just perfectly shaped.

He really wanted to think about all that silky skin he hadn't seen, but just as his mind started to wander, down the hall came the pathologist.

"What have you got, Billy?", asked David.

"Well, I definitely need to go over the reports on the other two victims, but, this wound was caused by a blade, unlike the rest of the wounds. If we can find the same mark on the other two, we'll have a pattern and probably a serial killer. You'll have to give me a couple of days."

"Get it to me by end of day tomorrow at the latest."

"O.K. Joe, I'll do my best."

With that, they left the morgue.

# Chapter 17

I went ahead and refilled my drink and sat back down in front of the fire Joe had built. The flames licked the thick, crackling logs. Between the heat of the fireplace, the ticking of the clock, and the smell of the fire, I was getting sleepy, however, I knew I needed to think. It was definitely getting harder to be around him. I knew he wanted to kiss me, and I certainly wanted him to, but, I also knew that the life with a cop would not be a good one. How do you watch him go to work everyday and not wonder if it will be the last time you ever see him?

Now, of course I realize that when your time is up, your time is up no matter what you do for a living, however, there are certainly some professions that put you in a higher risk category, and being a cop is one of them. I was truly afraid to fall in love with someone that could widow me at an early age.

I've never been good at marriage, and I'm not sure why. Maybe it was the wrong man, bad timing, or just the fact that I didn't have good role models for parents. I hate to argue, and I expect compromise and courtesy. If you break it admit it, if you use it replace it, and put things back the way you found them. No big deal, right? Well, guess what! Yes, it is a big deal. It's always the little things that break down a relationship.

You know they say that if a person is rude to the waiter or not respectful of their mother, that this is not a good person.

OK, so the problem is that Joe is passing all the tests! That was scaring me. He always seemed so gentle around me. I'm sure he can be a real ass, but, to me he was always careful to be gentle and soft. Boy, I really think I'm in trouble. I just can't let myself fall for a cop. That's right, it's not going to happen. There is definitely better husband material out there. Wait a minute I thought! Husband material! What the hell is wrong with me? I'm not looking for a husband! Shit, I'm going to bed. Obviously the booze has gone to my head!

"C'mon girls, let's go!"

# Chapter 18

I met with Mrs. Hawthorne at ten the next morning to go over my latest ideas. I also wanted to talk to her about the things I'd seen at the antique shop downtown.

She seemed in a giddy mood, almost like she wanted to spend anything to get what she wanted. So, when I started telling her about my trip to the antique shop, she jumped at the idea of crystal, silver, gold, anything I thought would be spectacular. She decided she really loved the very ornate, and chose the Duncan Phyfe pieces I had suggested.

I was truly relieved about not getting any hassle about my choices. I realize the average person doesn't study period furniture, and am always relieved when my client lets me do what I'm paid to do.

In the case of Mrs. Hawthorne's French bedroom, the sinuous curves in the wall panels produce an effect of dignified gaiety, tending slightly toward sentimental and feminine characteristics. Duncan Phyfe (1768-1854) is popularly considered the outstanding American cabinetmaker of the early 19th century. There is no doubt as to his remarkable ability; whether he is to be considered superior, however, to some of his predecessors or even to some of his contemporaries is open to question.

He came to America from Scotland as a young man, in 1784. After learning the trade of cabinet making in Albany, New York, he moved to New York City about 1790 and opened a shop of his own. His success was almost instantaneous, and although he died a disappointed man in 1854 at the age of 86, he left a distinct mark upon the industrial arts of America. His finest work was produced between 1795 and 1818, during which years he closely followed the Sheraton designs.

Thomas Sheraton, the third great name connected with English furniture design, ranks with Chippendale and Hepplewhite. Born about 1751, he was self-educated, became a preacher and a scholar, wrote religious tracts, studied mathematics, and tried his hand at almost everything.

He arrived in London from Stockton-on-Tees in Durham about 1790, published The Cabinet-Maker and Upholsterer's Drawing Book in 1791, and unquestionably designed much furniture that was made by other cabinetmakers.

Many of Sheraton's designs were for very small pieces of furniture suitable to the dressing room and boudoir.

We went over my proposals including the crystal chandlier for her bath, the contrast of the soft fabrics against the smooth darkness of the wood, and the accessories.

When I left it was obvious we were both excited.

As soon as I got home, I spread my notes across my work table. Now I had some serious decisions to make, place my orders and purchase the accessories.

# Chapter 19

Very satisfied with the results of my meeting with Mrs. H., and my completed list of "things to do", I got up from my work table noticing it was already getting dark.

I mixed myself a drink and quickly fed the girls. I also needed to start thinking about Christmas, I realized. With Mom and Dad gone, it would just be Dawn, Wayne and me. Thanksgiving was just three weeks away, and we had decided to have both holidays at my place. I took my drink and a note pad and headed for the veranda.

Dawn wanted me to cook the biggest turkey I could find so we'd have plenty of leftovers. We love to freeze the turkey in two cup containers to be used for turkey noodle soup, turkey tetrazzini, turkey and noodles, turkey stroganoff, turkey primavera, and lots of other yummy dishes. She'll bring the baked beans, breads, stuffing and appetizers. I'll do the potatoes, pie and cranberries. Of course, there will be plenty of cheese, crackers, cheese balls, dips and spreads, nuts, popcorn, cider and rum, and without a doubt, lots of wine.

I needed to give some thought to Christmas gifts, but Dawn is so easy to buy for it's really a snap, and Wayne loves anything Harley Davidson.

As I headed back in to refill my drink, I heard the phone ringing.

"I've got the most perfect Porterhouse steaks and a couple of bottles of wine," a sexy voice said, "you want to join me for dinner?"

"May I see your ID officer?"

"I'll show you anything you want, Ms. Fox," he purred.

"Oh, my!" I exclaimed with a chuckle. "May I bring anything?"

"How about your tooth brush?" he teased. "See you at eight." and hung up.

# Chapter 20

I took a long hot shower, washing my hair with the rich jasmine-scented shampoo and conditioner that Frederick Fekkai made up espeically for me, lathered twice with jasmine body shampoo, and after briskly toweling off, smoothed coordinating creamy lotion all over my body.

The last few days had been unseasonably warm, so I dressed in very soft pink cotton cuffed shorts, as my tan was still a beautiful creamy color, a matching top with wine bottles and wine glasses happily dancing across it with beads and stones that shined, and soft pink sandals that also had beads and stones that adorned them. To this I added fun pink ear bobs, then twisted my hair up into a pink clasp.

He had rented a cottage just down the beach from me, and as I approached I could see him through the kitchen French doors. He had on khaki shorts, a polo shirt and dock shoes. He was mixing something, very engrossed in his work, so I snuck up the stairs from the beach and rapped sharply on the glass, watching him jump and throw the utensils he was using into the air. He screamed something, then muttered something else while he opened the door for me.

"Awfully jumpy for a cop, aren't you?" I snickered.

"Cute," was his only reply.

"What are you making?" I inquired.

"Caesar salad, so why don't you mix us a drink?" he glowered.

I spied a cocktail bar at the end of the kitchen and proceeded to fix a couple of Black Velvet's on the rocks. When I handed him his, he pushed me against the counter, and I felt the hardness of him against me. He lowered his head and his mouth came down over mine with a possessiveness that surprised me. I kissed him back feeling the intense heat, and then suddenly he pulled away, almost like he needed to get that out of his system. I should have felt assaulted, however I felt wonderful instead.

He went back to preparations of the salad and asked me how I liked my steak.

"Rare, or medium rare, depending on the chef," I replied.

He glanced sideways at me, and resumed his duties. "So, just what brought you to this area?" he asked.

"Well, I was born in Iowa, studied in New York, and decided if I were to ever make any money I needed to be where people loved to spend money. I've worked very hard to be the very best I can, and I am lucky to have an excellent reputation throughout the community of the privileged."

At this point the salad was done and he went to the refrigerator, pulled out two beautiful thick steaks, and headed for the grill. I could smell the baked potatoes in the oven, I picked up my bourbon and headed out onto the patio right behind him. He threw the steaks onto the flaming grill, and smiled.

He was so confident, so sexy, without even trying. It was almost like he didn't care what you thought of him. He knew who he was and didn't care if anybody liked him or not.

He had a patio table set for dinner and even had all the flatware in the right place! He reached over and flipped a switch on a CD player, and for the second time tonight he surprised me by playing classical music. A timer went off on the stove and I offered to get the potatoes and salad. He had wine open and breathing, and we sat down to a wonderful meal.

We talked about some of my clients and some funny things that have happened to me over the years, like the time I submitted my bill to a clients husband, or so I thought. Turns out the guy is her lover, takes one look at the amount and says to me, "she isn't that good in bed," hands the bill back to me and walks off. I damn near died. He had a few funny stories of his own so we sat there enjoying the night and a second bottle of wine.

Finally we got up to carry the dishes into the kitchen, and before I knew what was happening he gathered me into his arms. He slowly kissed me and his lips were warm and moist. His arms were strong around me and I felt totally protected. Then suddenly he scooped me up in his arms and carried me straight to his bedroom. He laid me gently on the bed and laid down beside me. His kisses became more passionate and I could feel his body grow hard with need. He carefully undressed me, and then almost tore off his own clothing. He was rock hard and had a huge, thick cock. I felt the warm moistness of my own desire as he slid smoothly inside me. He was an expert lover, gentle and rough, and knew all the right places and moves.

I fell into a light soft sleep with my head on his chest. I'm not sure how much time passed, but I finally sat up and said that I had to get home for the girls. He said he'd walk me. He put his arm around me as we walked, and it all felt so natural. He kissed me tenderly at my door and headed back to his place.

# Chapter 21

At headquarters geographic profilers, who use computer grids and their own logic to try to figure out where a serial killer lives or works based on where he kills, have said the killer must be following a geographical pattern because such killers do. Also, by noting the hours of each murder, it can give insight where the perp might work. So far, they weren't coming up with much.

"Billy from the morgue is on the phone Christensen!" one of the officers yelled.

Christensen grabbed the phone, "what do you have, Billy?"

"Well, David, I've gone over the other vic's files and after closer examination, I can see how it was missed before. I don't know what it might mean, but all three of these women and trace amounts of pasta undigested in their stomachs.

"What about the knife wound?"

"Not a knife wound. Could have happened by accident earlier in the day. She could have run into a metal shelf bracket or anything sharp enough to break the skin. It was a superficial wound."

"Thanks, Billy. Keep me posted." with that he hung up the phone and immediately punched in Fredosa's number.

"Joe here."

"We've found a connection."

"I'll be right there."

As he raced to the station, he couldn't stop thinking about Madeline. God what a woman. So sexual, responsive, eager to please, and totally uninhibited. She just had a natural thirst for sex, everything any man could long for. She's bright, funny, extremely independent, sexy, delicious and God did she smell good! Plus, she always looked stunning. And now he had to wonder once this case is solved what happens to the relationship. At this point, he was entirely ready to proceed full speed ahead. But, what if she wasn't? He'd make a complete fool of himself. Man, he couldn't let that happen no matter what! So what now? Did he need to act like no big deal to what just happened! Shit, he thought, why does this need to be so complicated?

He wondered what she was doing right now. He could still smell her, for God's sake. Maybe it was just his memory, whatever, but she definitely was intoxicating.

As he thought about it he wasn't sure he liked this one little bit. He'd always been in control of these kind of situations. Women usually threw themselves at him, but not her, no way! He practically had to cuff her at first! Maybe that was it. He just wasn't used to having to make the moves. It truly seemed like it had been a long time for her, unlike these women that claim it has been so long, whatever! A guy could tell. But Madeline never claimed that, but he could tell it had been a very long time, and he wondered why. She must have been very hurt or something. It certainly wasn't because she was homely! He couldn't imagine any man not being attracted to her!

He was just so taken with her. She's a very special person, he thought. He'd never been with anyone like her. She really has it all going for her, and he wanted to be in her life. He had never considered marriage, until now. He had to stop thinking about her, his cock was getting hard again!

## Chapter 22

As I sat in my big kitchen sipping coffee, I reflected on last night. He is very tender and compassionate, but he's still a cop. I just don't understand how they think. They really don't make that much money and they will kill people. It has to be a macho thing. You know, it seems that they don't really try to solve crimes, but are more interested in writing tickets to speeders. When you think about it, these speeders are good people that pay their taxes and live normal lives, but sometimes get in a hurry to meet all their obligations. These are people that hold down jobs, pay their bills and make contributions to worthy causes. Just the law abiding citizen these guys go after. What's up with that! What about the drug labs, drug pushers and all the dope heads out there? It's not right!

Oh well, I've got more important things to think about anyway! I picked up the phone to order Mrs. H's fabrics, then I needed to go downtown to purchase the accessories from "Needful Treasures" for her bath. I needed to put Joe Fredosa out of my mind.

Once my orders were placed, I jumped into the shower. I decided on red jeans and matching jacket, with a white tee with navy stars and matching accessories. I grabbed a check from the business check book and headed out the door. I would like to open an account, but because her business was brand new and they didn't know me from Adam, I wanted to cover my bases.

Once I got there, I introduced myself to the owner, Ellen White. She was very appreciative of my purchases and was happy to start an account for me once she realized who my clients were. I immediately liked her, she must have been around fifty, with beautiful silver hair and smooth skin.

She walked with me through the mansion taking notes on the items I wanted. Completing this we went to her office and I gave her the address for delivery and we decided upon a time so I could be there to receive the inventory. It ended up being quite an impressive purchase and she invited me to the little tea room for a glass of wine.

She said she was widowed last year and really missed her husband because he had been her best friend all twenty-five years of their marriage. She started Needful Treasures to keep herself occupied, and it truly had helped with the loneliness. How lucky she was, I thought, to have had such a wonderful relationship. It made me wonder if I would ever consider marriage again. Probably not, my life is full and happy just the way it is.

Just then Ellen was saying she has two grown sons named Jake and John. Jake was CEO of a large law firm and John was a doctor. She was apparently very proud of them. They were both in their twenties and single.

We had a lovely conversation, and promised to meet next week to have dinner.

# Chapter 23

When I got home there were several calls to return to potential clients. At my worktable I made several appointments and wrote them in my Daytimer. I looked at my watch and it was four o'clock. What next? I decided I needed some fresh air, grabbed the girls and their leashes, kicked off my shoes and headed for the beach.

It's always a beautiful walk especially in the late afternoon when lights were coming on in the elegant homes of my neighbors. I waived to Jack who was creating another colorful canvas on his veranda. Jack is a very well liked local artist with a flair for the exotic. Just then his companion, Michael, came out carrying two martini's. Both men looked like centerfolds for GQ Magazine, what a waste, I thought. Michael had the military look, where as Jack's signature black ponytail lent to his artsy look.

What to do for dinner, I thought. Well, whatever, I sure wasn't having dessert like last night! That could become addicting! I considered "Tony's" but, decided I needed to have fish. After last nights red meat, I certainly didn't need pasta. I didn't want to get fat, for crying out loud! Yes, it would be orange roughy, a salad and rice. A bourbon while preparing and a glass of wine with dinner. Now that that's settled, I thought, my next consideration was any preparations before tomorrow's two appointments.

My first appointment was with the Thoroughgood's. I knew the house well. With its sharp gables, large chimney, and small-paned windows reminiscent of its English ancestry, it stands today as the oldest brick house in America.

The second appointment was with Mrs. Jefferson. This home was built during the Federal Period and Greek Revival 1790 - 1850. Typical of this era were columns capped with one of the three famous Greek orders, i.e., Doric, Ionic, or Corinthian. Columns also appeared inside, separating rooms and supporting mantels. Pediments were placed over doorways, windows, and fireplaces; reeding, bead and reel, egg and dart, the urn, and all manner of classical decorations were employed both inside and out.

O.K., after thinking about it, I felt I knew enough going in without any research. So, back home because I was ready for that cocktail!

## Chapter 24

My first appointment was at ten. Mrs. Thoroughgood was a very charming woman. All height and posture, she was actually like a thoroughbred horse. Very elegant and very proper. We are to do her "receiving parlour" and her gourmet kitchen. Most of her pieces were very old and priceless. This will be a challenge, I thought. But, I love a challenge! The receiving parlour, where her guests are first taken for cocktails would be the easier of the two to handle, however, the gourmet kitchen would take a lot more time and qualifying.

I asked if her chef could join us, and I started on my list of questions. I needed to understand just how extensive the kitchen was used, for how many guests, buffets or sit down formal dinners, late night suppers, brunch's, what kind of parties, what appliances did we need to accommodate fresh fish, fruits and vegetable storage, a possible locker for meats, the hanging and drying of specialty items, etc.

After two hours I felt I could proceed without question. This would be a large undertaking, and a very expensive one for the Thoroughgood's, but I knew that wasn't a problem. I asked her to give me a week, and I would make another appointment with her to go over my ideas. She seemed pleased, and I left with just enough time to get to the Jefferson's.

Mrs. Jefferson was a slight woman of about seventy. I had heard a lot about the lavish parties she threw. She had a quiet understatement about her, however her huge diamonds looked like they could break her delicate hands.

At Mrs. Jefferson's we were doing the dining room and the study for her husband. He, a retired doctor just waived the whole thing off saying he liked his study the way it was. But, it was obvious that if the Mrs. wanted it, he gave it to her. He looked at her with such a tenderness in his eyes it made my heart ache.

I asked him if he would be willing to talk to me about his favorite things, colors and needs. He was a sweet man and was very helpful. He liked the "club" look with lots of plaids, and a very male atmosphere.

Next to the dining room.

Mrs. Jefferson had kept with the history and time of the home by using Federal pieces in the dining room. Federal was not an ornate period and she now wanted fluff. The Federal period, 1795 to 1830, covers the era between the Colonial and Victorian in America. Some authorities divide this into two periods: The Federal (1780-1800) and American Empire (1800-1830). It is dominated by the work of Duncan Phyfe, who set the pace for all other craftsmen. Although the chief source of inspiration was French Empire, much 18th century and Colonial influence is evident.

However, upon my qualifying questions, I knew for sure that Mrs. Jefferson wanted the Victorian look. Of course, this is my specialty!

Victorian is the name given the furniture design created during the reign of Queen Victoria (1837-1901), a style developed in England and enthusiastically copied in America. This was an attempt to achieve both excellence of construction and a superiority of decoration, designed to please the primness, affectation and stodgy respectability of the times. It was usually a huge, substantially built and very often clumsy style, never sure of itself. The entire output of the Victorian period, however, is not to be condemned. Occasional pieces of great beauty were produced, and several efforts were made with variable success to break away from the pall of esthetic stagnation.

I loved working with the Victorian fabrics and left her with a promise to call within a week with my ideas.

Whew, what a day! I had a lot to think about and needed to get to work. By the time I got home, it was mid afternoon. Good, I thought, I've got some of the daylight left to put together my ideas. I was really excited! I pulled out some research books and got down to business!

When I finally looked up from my work, it was getting dark outside so I straightened my work table just a bit and headed for the kitchen to feed the girls.

Now, what for dinner for me? I opened the huge refrigerator and peered inside. There I found a meaty chicken breast, fresh asparagus, and to that I would make some seasoned potato wedges. I put the chicken breast in a baking dish, covered it in Italian dressing and preheated the oven. I scrubbed two medium sized potatoes and cut them into wedges. Then I mixed olive oil, paprika, garlic salt and chili powder together. I coated the potatoes in the oil mixture and placed them on a baking sheet. By that time the oven had reached proper temperature and I slid the two baking dishes in side by side.

So, now I have forty-five minutes until that gets done. I cleaned the asparagus and got out my double-boiler. Now with that ready to be steamed, I opened a bottle of wine and lit the fire.

*Blood & Wine*

OK, Thanksgiving is less than a week away, so I grabbed the pen and paper off the little oak table and started making notes. Tomorrow I'd shop for the food I would need. That will give the turkey the two days required to thaw in the refrigerator. Well, to think of it, it may take three because of the size. I'll pick up fresh potatoes and cranberries. I'll make a pumpkin and a peach pie, because Wayne's favorite is peach. Let's do the traditional mashed potatoes, maybe add a little garlic, and creamy turkey gravy from the drippings. I'll need to pick up more Glenfeddich for Wayne, and as always, there's plenty of white and red wines for Dawn and myself. I had a fairly standing order with the local liquor store, however they always threw in some new and different ones for me to try, and just billed me on a monthly basis. They also delivered and the young man would uncase and fill my wine racks for me. He usually had a little snack that I would make for him while he was here, and he took the empty boxes with him when he left so the mess went with him.

At a spur of the minute, I decided to invite Comander Fredosa and Detective Christensen and picked up the tiny cordless on the table. I had the numbers right there on their business cards, and dialed Joe first. He accepted with thanks, and David said he was grateful for the invitation, just being recently divorced he thought he'd be eating a Swanson turkey dinner. I remembered his grocery basket and had to stifle a giggle.

By now my dinner was almost ready, so I ran cold water into my pan and turned the gas up high. I took the chicken breast out of the oven and placed the dish on the cutting board. It need to rest so the juices would redistribute throughout the meat before cutting. The potatoes were about five minutes from being done, and now my water was boiling, so I added the asparagus to the top of the double boiler, pinched some kosher salt from the crock that always sat beside the cooktop, and sprinkled it over the asparagus. I put the lid on the pot, started gathering my plate and utensils, and refilled my wine glass. I ate in front of the fire, and savored the juicy chicken, the potatoes were crispy on the outside and perfect on the inside, and the asparagus was crisp tender, just the way it was supposed to be.

After I cleaned up and refilled my glass of wine, I called Dawn and told her I'd invited Joe and David. She said that was fine with her, so we proceeded to go over the menu.

We hung up after about half an hour and I was exhausted, so I headed to bed.

# Chapter 25

I woke up the next morning to a bright beautiful crisp autumn day. I just love the fall and went happily to my kitchen to make coffee. I had a lot to do today and needed to stay organized.

I went over my shopping list again, just to be sure, then I picked up the phone and called the florist. I ordered fresh fall arrangements for Dawn and Wayne's bedroom and bath, a larger one for the top of the bombe chest in my bedroom, and a low spread for the dining room table. At the last minute I decided on a narrow arrangement for the fire place mantle, one that would hold candles. More mums, this time for inside, to bunch together throughout the house for color.

I grabbed my coffee, and went upstairs to take a shower. I let the heads blast me with the hottest water I could stand, lathered with L'Occitante shea butter and honeysuckle soap, rinsed with a cooler temperature, then towelled off. After wandering around in my walk-in closet, I decided on heavy cotton shorts with a matching long sleeved top in a deep green, braided with a golden cord and small, corded golden tassles on the pocket flaps, paired with buttery soft, leather green flats that matched exactly, and gold accessories. Luckily, when I found the shoes, there was a matching handbag. They had cost me a pretty penny, but so what. One must look her best at all times! I pulled my hair into a pony tail and wrapped it with gold cording. Satisfied with my reflection, I grabbed my list and headed out the door.

I wouldn't have to lug floral arrangements, as they were being delivered early the morning before Dawn arrived, so all there was to shop for were the groceries I needed. "Franks," was the local market I used, and it covered what seemed as acres. There isn't anything you won't find here, and he carried all the exotic foods, oils, vinegars, herbs, spices, cheeses, and wines you could ever dream of. They just billed me once a month, so it made things go much faster if you were in a hurry, and today I was. I knew the store like the back of my hand, gathered what I needed, plus a little more, and got out of there. It was starting to fill up with pre-Thanksgiving shoppers, and I wanted no part of the crowd!

I decided to stop for a sandwich at a trendy little place called "Finger It Out." They specialized in unique sandwiches that you could eat there or order to-go. Very fun ladies and a gent between the ages of sixty and seventy ran it. They were always such a hoot! The white haired gent, Richard, scurried about clearing tables and serving sandwiches. The special today was a thinly sliced, honey roasted ham, swiss cheese with a dill dressing and sliced red onion, served on a lightly toasted Hawaiian sweet bread. I ordered that along with a glass of Pinot

Noir, VI N DE PAYS D'OC, French Reserve.

While waiting for my lunch, I pulled out my new Stuart Woods book, found my bookmark, and started reading while sipping my wine. When my sandwich arrived, I thanked Richard and took a bite. As usual, it was delicious. The ham had the desired honey flavor, the swiss was melted and pouring over the sides and the dill dressing was fresh and homemade. The Hawaiian bread was a prefect package for the fresh ingredients, and the red onion gave it the extra kick it needed.

When I left the restaurant, I headed to the hairdresser for my appointment. I needed a trim, and was scheduled for a manicure and a pedicure. A little pampering is always in order, especially when you're expecting a house full of guests!

When I got home, I unloaded the groceries from the cooler I always kept in my trunk of my car, carried them inside and stashed everything away. Whew! I dropped into my favorite lounge chair on the veranda for a tiny rest. I watched the sun on its mid-day descent with a contented sigh. I kicked off my shoes and both girls jumped into my lap giving me happy kisses. I was excited about the upcoming Holidays, and the opportunity to have the celebrations at my place.

The food was always wonderful and the dress always casual. However, with Joe and David here this year, I would jazz it up a bit! Mary was due in tomorrow, and while she cleaned, I would bake pies. Since fall is my favorite time of year, I would dig out all my beautiful pieces to decorate with. I will have Mary work with me, so she can put pieces away while I bring out my fall treasurers.

I was still full from my wonderful lunch, so I decided to mix a strong kahlua and cream, feed my girls, and go upstairs to run myself a hot bath. Shaking Flois Lily of the Valley liberally into the steaming water, I breathed in the cloud of fragrant scent, as I slid slowly into the water. I lit candles and dimmed the lights. I sipped my drink and laid my head against the edge of the tub. I guess I was almost asleep when the girls burst into the room chasing each other. I sat up, took a sip and smiled at their energy. I scrubbed and polished my skin, and wrapped in a fluffy terry monogramed robe, slipped into matching terry slippers and left the bath with my drink.

I decided to watch the ocean, for what might be the last time of solitude I'd have for the next few days. The breeze was fragrant, the ocean swayed as if moving to the music of a lullaby, there was a full moon, and I took it all in.

Finally, overcome by exhaustion, I headed to bed with my girls. I slept like a baby.

The next morning I woke early and refreshed. I jumped out of bed, put on some sweats and headed for the kitchen to make coffee. I ground my favorite coffee beans, cinnamon macadamia nut, splashed cream into my cup and readied myself for the day.

Mary arrived at her usual time of nine, and I filled her in on what I had in mind for the day. As always, she was in agreement, and got started with the dusting.

I went to the attic, found the boxes marked "fall," and opened them up. Everything was wrapped in tissue and clean from last years packing efforts. I kept baskets in the attic for the purpose of transferring pieces to different floors, and started to load a large one. The next two hours were a flurry of exchanging this for that, but the outcome was stunning. While Mary put the finishing touches on the cleaning end, I headed for the kitchen.

I checked the turkey and it was thawing per schedule, so I began with my pie crusts. I had fresh peaches and my special pumpkin for the pies. I was ready to go, however there must be some lunch for Mary and me, to keep our energy flowing. Mary was always on a diet, however, she never turned down anything I made for us. I always tried to fix salads or something light so she wouldn't feel guilty. I decided on cobb salad, with sliced tomatoes, olives, red onion, hard-boiled eggs, shredded cheese and ham, served with a light ranch dressing. She had iced tea and I had water with freshly squeezed lemon. I served it with crusty rolls and butter, and we ate eagerly.

Back to work! I loaded the dishwasher, cleaned up the kitchen and started on my pies. The day went smoothly, and by the time Mary left everything was in order. I'd put the turkey in the oven tomorrow late morning, scrub potatoes, get appetizers in order and ready myself for the floral arrangement delivery.

I needed a drink! I lit the fire in the big kitchen fireplace, splashed whiskey in a tumbler with ice, and breathed diet coke over it.

I literly fell into the chair. By tomorrow at this time, everything should be in full swing! It was going to be fun, and I was really looking forward to seeing Joe again, and also showing him what a wonderful hostess I can be.

You know, I'm not even sure why I thought that. Cops don't have dinner parties, do they? Oh well, I really didn't care. I do, and that's all that mattered.

I decided to skip dinner and take a shower, knowing I'd fall asleep in the tub and probably drown. Tomorrow was going to be a big day, and I crawled into the stiff, clean sheets with a moan of delight. I was asleep before my head hit the pillow.

# Chapter 26

The sun shown brightly through the sheer panels covering the bedroom windows. I awoke with a yawn and streached lazily. I jumped out of bed, threw on my softest sweats and headed to the kitchen.

The flower arrangements would arrive soon and I wanted to be ready. I started freshly ground mocha beans in the coffee maker and went back upstairs to make the bed. Just as I finished, the door bell rang. As I ran to the back door, Bloomin' Wacky, who knew to always deliver there, had three young men carrying stunning arrangements up the porch steps. I flung open the door and exclaimed 'Happy Thanksgiving!' to the delivery boys. They all knew me well, because they have been here many times before, so I directed each one of them where to go with the different arrangements.

When they had brought everything in, I offered them coffee, but they declined saying they had many deliveries ahead of them. I tipped them generously and they headed on their way.

Everything looked spectacular! I sipped my coffee touring the floors.

It was just shortly after eight thirty, and the house was in perfect condition for my guests. I double checked the guest bath for towels, bath sugars, oils, shampoos and lotions. I always stocked a variety so my guests had many to choose from.

Back to the kitchen. I expected my guests to arrive around two this afternoon, so I set the turkey out to bring it up to room temperature. I always make the stuffing separate from the turkey, because I believe it makes the turkey dry, as you have to bake it longer to get the dressing done. Anyway, not to worry about that, because Dawn is bringing the dressing. She likes to make her specialty with dried cranberries. Speaking of cranberries, I'm making a new and easy cranberry dish with a twist! All you do is take a can of whole berry cranberries and the same size can of applesauce. Mix them together in a sauce pan, and just heat it up! That's it! Easy and fast, so there's more time to spend with your guests.

Now for the potatoes. Not your traditional mashed with turkey gravy, too much last minute work, I decided! Instead we'll have my famous Creamy Escalloped Potatoes. I scrubbed and sliced five cups of unpeeled potatoes into a large shiny metal bowl. In a smaller bowl I added one can of cream of chicken soup with one-half cup of whole milk, one medium chopped onion and salt and pepper to-taste. I poured my mixture into the large bowl of potatoes and mixed well. Then into a buttered casserole, dotted it with butter, put the lid on and shoved it into the already bulging refrigerator. It only needed to bake for one hour at 375* covered, and uncovered for an additional 15 minutes. It's easy with two wall ovens, the turkey will go in one, and the potatoes in the other. So when the potatoes have been in the oven for approximately fifteen minutes, I'll take the turkey out, flip it over onto its breast so the juices will flow throughout the meat and let it set for at least half an hour before carving. I'll get one of the guys to do the carving!

As I sipped my coffee, I sliced cheeses, and assembled green and black olives and pickles onto my favorite appetizer platter, covered it and into the refrigerator it went. Next I made a creamy cold shrimp butter to spread on the assorted crackers that would be piled high in a tall, jumbo margarita glass. I set out the cream cheese so it would warm up to room temperature. That's for my hot crab dip. I chose some pretty antique leaf shaped glass bowls for nuts, and arranged everything nicely on the center island. I'll fill the bowls at the last minute, so everything is fresh. Next I got out some festive fall linen napkins and small glass plates, along with little forks, spreaders and serving spoons. Then I arranged brightly colored fall leaves that were made from a special heavy paper, making them look very real, along with wooden acorns, baby boo pumpkins and funny looking gourds. It looked wonderful!

Next, the dining room table. I have many sets of china and flatware, but today I'm using my bright white plates and gold flatware. I especially like the contrast against the crisp fall linens. Water and wine goblets next, and deep green taper candles in my moms antique crystal candleobras, to be placed near the elegant fall centerpiece. It was long and conversationally low, in rich fall oranges, deep greens and warm browns, along with blood red berries, the florist had artfully arranged everyting in a heavy oblong black marble dish.

OK, everything is done so I headed to the shower. I decided on an emerald green heavy cotton pant-set. The top was a long tunic style that buttoned down the front with gold trimmed diamond-like buttons. It was accented with more of these diamonds, but in various shapes. I then slipped into clear acrylic sandals that were accented with matching diamond studs across the top. Four-carat diamond studs in my ears, and I was ready.

Back in the kitchen I built a huge fire, assembled wine glasses, selected a crisp white from the wine refrigerator, and popped the cork. After sampling the wine, I got the turkey into the oven. I needed a little snack and went to the ole' sub-zero for a peek. There were coldcuts, so I quickly assembled a sandwich, sat in front of the fire with my wine and realized that this would be the last time today I'd have a quiet moment. That was OK, I was really looking forward to our little celebration.

After I ate, I started filling bowl of nuts, heaped crackers into the large goblet, got the appetizer tray from the refrigerator, set out the shrimp butter and got started on my Hot Crabmeat Spread. In a saucepan went two blocks of cream cheese, one-half cup half and half, one small onion chopped fine, two minced cloves of garlic, some mayonnaise, horseradish, lemon juice, Worcestershire sauce, ten drops hot pepper sauce and two cans crabmeat. Now, it just needed to heat slowly and it would be ready.

Precisely at two, the doorbell rang, and there stood Commander Fredosa and Dective Christensen smiling widely. Just then Dawn and Wayne pulled in.

"Hey, will you guys help Wayne carry things in?" I asked.

"Sure!" they said in unison.

When we got everyting carried in and settled, I started pouring glasses of wine for all.

We munched, drank wine and told lies. The turkey was jucy and tender and everything was done to perfection.

By nine o'clock everyone had left except Joe. We sat in the kitchen in front of the fire reflecting on the day.

"Madeline, I have never had a Thanksgiving like this one in my life. You make everything so special, and I just want you to know I thank you very much for including me today."

"Of course, Joe, it was really fun!"

He got out of his chair, bent over me and kissed me full on my mouth. He then pulled me out of my chair and wrapped his arms around me. I could feel he was aroused as his mouth came down over mine once again. His kisses became more and more passionate and my legs were threatening to give out on me. I pulled away and said "take me to bed" to which he replied "I thought you'd never ask!"

Joe had a 'perfect package' and was a passionate lover. He knew how to please a woman completely. His hands moved expertly over my body until I thought I'd scream. Just then he swiftly entered me. I exploded almost immediately, but he just kept thrusting into me. I came over and over again, until he, almost out of his mind with need bucked hard and groaned.

We fell apart exhausted and exhilarated all at once. After a few minutes of panting, I rolled over and snuggled in close to him and fell immediately asleep.

Joe left early the next morning and I jumped into the shower. I had a busy day ahead of me, and I needed to get started.

I made coffee, fed the girls and headed out to get my errands done.

When I got home there was an invitation stuck in the door jamb to a party at Jack and Michael's tonight. Impromptu. Very normal for my neighbors to throw together a bash at the last moment. Don't get me wrong, there will be nothing thrown together about the party. Everybody has on-call caterers, butlers, bartenders, rent-all coordinators and musicians. Even some magicians and strippers make the list!

Well, of course I'd go. What to wear! Again my thoughts went to Dawn. Man, I just hate it when she's right. I knew it would be a black tie affair, so I chose a black sheath that opened up in the middle to show my midriff and waistline, with one shoulder completely exposed and the other only sporting a rhinestone strap. The rhinestones picked up again at my thigh and ran the length of the gown, which was slit from the floor to my upper thigh. Rhinestone ear bobs and matching evening bag, piece of cake!

I fed the girls, jumped into the shower and got dressed. I decided to catch my hair in a rhinestone clasp, spritzed myself with Opium and left. I decided to drive, because I didn't want to show up covered with sand. I knew Michael would have a hissy fit if there was sand on all that white carpeting!

The house was ablaze with lights and candles. The pool was lit with hundreds of floating candles and the waiters were everywhere in their black scant tuxedo's. Jack and Michael liked to employ mostly men, so the normal French maids were no where to be found!

I accepted a glass of champagne from one of the scantily clad, buffed up waiters, wondering if he also felt the chill of the night air. I greeted my hosts, and was surprised to see Tony across the room.

I glanced around the huge room. I've been here many times before, but it always amazed me how much white there was. Basically everything was white, the only color to be found was in candles and throw pillows, and that was a pale lavender.

There was lots of glass, floor to ceiling, for breathtaking views of the ocean.

The buffet was extravagant, as I expected, and I fixed a plate of oysters on the half shell, fresh shrimp, Bulgari caviar, and a combination of fresh tuna, crab, shrimp, clams, and scallops done in a light sauce. Fresh steamed lobster was heaped on a platter. There were an array of cheeses, including brie, toast points, loaves of sour dough bread, herring in shrimp sauce, herring in cream sauce, huge bowls of fresh strawberries and grapes. The table looked like it would groan with the weight if it could!

I was surprised to see several people I didn't know. Fortunately, that doesn't happen to me very often.

There were three men in particular that had somewhat of a shady look to them. They were talking with several of the art gallery owners. No wives were present at this conversation, and it just had a funny feel to me.

They had a live band that played a variety of music, and finally Michael sat down at the white Baby Grand and played several sing-along tunes that were loved by all.

I was surprised that Tony hadn't yet talked to me. It was so unlike him. Maybe he had a girlfriend with him and didn't want to be seen talking to other women. Strange though, we're just friends if that. Why would he ignore me here when he acts like he does at the restaurant?

I decided to head outside for some fresh air. On my way out I nabbed a fresh glass of champagne. The evening was beautiful and the floating candles put off a lot of heat that took some of the night chill away.

Another bar was set up out here, and gallons of champagne certainly were flowing.

I spotted Gabrielle and headed over to speak to her. Gabrielle is a sculpture. Very talented and very well liked. She is probably sixty, with long gray hair that she wears in a pony tail high upon her head. Her clothes are always very flamboyant, and tonight she had on a red and orange concoction that appeared to be hundreds of yards of flowing fabric. She is nearly six feet tall and rail thin. I swear she smokes five packs of cigarettes a day! Her craggy voice sounds like she has smoked Camel's all her life and she drinks straight whiskey.

Of course, there she was among the champagne drinkers with her cigarette and tumbler of whiskey on the rocks!

She was talking to a striking silver haired man, with her arms gesturing excitedly in the air, while cigarette ashes flew everywhere. I even saw some of the whiskey slosh over the edge of the crystal tumbler. What a hoot! Good thing she wasn't inside! Michael would have flipped out over that thick white carpeting!

As I approached, she exclaimed, "Madeline! How good to see you, dear! Have you met our newcomer, Mack Lawson?"

I held out my hand to shake Mack's, but instead he kissed it, just after he gave me the once over. I felt naked. He then turned it palm up and kissed the inside. I withdrew my hand, and felt an intense heat engulf me.

"Oh, Mack," Gabrielle cooed, "stop teasing her, she's sweet!"

"She doesn't look sweet in that dress!" he retorted.

"Well," I said breathlessly, "it's nice to meet you, Mack, I think."

We all had a good laugh and I asked Mack what brought him to our little paradise.

"Actually, I was looking for the likes of you!" To which we all had another good laugh. I did notice that Mack had his hand over the top of his glass, so that Gabrielle's ashes didn't end up in his drink. Smart move, I thought.

"Seriously," I said.

"Well, I was looking for a place to retire, and did my research. This place sounded like just what I was looking for. So, here I am."

"What kind of business did you retire from?" I asked.

"Diamonds. I owned a diamond mine and specialized in custom made jewelry."

"Wow, I'm impressed." I said.

"I noticed you are wearing some very exquisite pieces, Madeline."

The pieces he was referring to were ones I rarely took off. They consisted of two David Yurman sterling silver jeweled solid bracelets, a diamond and ruby bracelet, a twenty something carat blue topaz and another of similar size amethyst bracelets.

I had on my two and one-half carat marquis diamond set in a heavy gold custom band, and my 29 carat blue topaz ring that is surround by baguette diamonds.

"Thanks, Mack, just stuff I've bought for myself."

"Well, now I'm impressed!" he exclaimed. "And what do you do?"

To this Gabrielle chimed in, "Oh, Madeline is an interior decorator with a flair that is truly exquisite!"

"Thank you, Gabrielle." I replied.

"Oh, my!" she exclaimed. "There would be Gregory, I must see him!" and off she went.

"May I buy you another drink?" Mack asked.

"Sure, why not." I said.

We sat near the pool for a long time talking about diamonds and gem stones, and I told him I bought my first diamond ring when I was twenty one years old. There was a jewelry store that I visited almost everyday, and the first was a cluster of nice sized stones on a double roped gold band that cost me $1,500.00. The jewelry store, Newton's, has long since been out of business, but I put down $100.00, and signed a contract to pay the rest within twelve months at no interest. Once I paid off that ring I got another one, then another. We both hooted at the no interest, and decided that those days were definitely gone!

After several of the guests had fallen drunkenly into the pool, I decided it was time to go home.

It had been a wonderful evening, and I bid farewell to my hosts, which were totally plowed, and headed out the door. As I headed to my car, I heard some shuffling and turned to look behind me. All at once this force rammed into me and I felt this stinky rag shoved over my nose and mouth, then everything went dark.

## Chapter 26

When I woke up I felt the cold cement beneath me. My hands and feet were bound by what I though might be rope. Where was I? Who had done this to me? I didn't want to make a noise, not knowing if my abductor was near me, but, I needed to figure out where I was! It was complete and utter black darkness.

I tried to rest, but I could hear the scurry of the rats around me. I curled around myself, I guess they call this the fetal position, and started to pray! What to do? My babies were at home and they needed me. I needed to keep a clear head! Man, I wish I'd worn my flannel p.j.'s! I was so cold!

What am I going to do? I had to try to think. My head hurt, had I fallen? Had I had a car accident? No, I would be in the hospital if I'd had. It was so hard to think, my head felt foggy. I felt very groggy and must have dozed in and out of sleep. When I woke up again there was enough light that I could see the lighthouse looming above me. My mind shreeked, "Oh no, I'm in an abandoned lighthouse and nobody will ever find me!"

I needed to calm down and keep a clear head. If I was going to get out of here alive, I'd need to make a plan. But first, I needed to know who had done this to me!

It felt like hours before I heard the closing of a door. I faked being asleep. I wasn't sure what to expect. I watched a figure approach.

Oh, my God, it was Tony! "Tony, Tony," I exclaimed! "I'm so glad to see you! Please help me!"

"Aw, Mia Fox, I sorry I can not do that."

"But, I don't understand, Tony. You are my friend." Right then I remembered my Mother and Sister telling me that you never have a true friend.

"No more, I sad to say. You just like the others now. You not pure anymore, because you fuck the cop. Now you spoil. You ruin everything I care for you, and I must kill you. I be more gentle with you, Mia. The others laughed at me, a mama's boy. But not you, you respect me, I so sad you spoil you. Now, I bring you some real dinner, pasta! You eat, I feed you."

"Please, Tony, I'm so cold."

"Yes, I see you wear whore dress in front of whole party!"

"Please, Tony, don't do this."

"You shut you face, and eat my wonderful pasta!"

I tried to swallow the food he shoved into my mouth and almost gagged.

"Oh, what you no like? You die hungry then."

With that, he left.

What to do? Think. You've got to think!

# Chapter 27

"Eee gads, Jack, what a mess!"

"Oh, but Michael, what a great party!" Jack winced holding his head with both hands. "We'll just call a service to come in and clean up."

As he walked to the phone he noticed Madeline's car still in the drive. "Did Madeline go home with someone, Michael?"

"Not that I remember, but I hardly remember her leaving." Michael replied. "Let's call her place."

"No answer. I think we should call the Police."

"Good idea, Jack."

Commander Fredosa and Detective Christensen arrived within minutes and a seemingly highly agitated Fredosa, shouted questions at Jack and Michael.

"Look," Jack exclaimed, "we're not sure if she left with someone or not. We can't tell you exactly what time she left because we weren't paying attention to the time, OK?"

Joe muttered something under his breath. "David, check her car for keys or any kind of clue, and then we'll go over to her place and see what we can find there. Thanks for nothing guys."

"Well," Michael swooned, "she did look very hot in that gown, which barely covered her. Barely is right," he giggled.

Jack shot him a filthy look, at which point Michael fussed around straightening up.

This entirely enraged Joe. He tried not to let it show, however, David caught it.

"Let's go, David." and they slammed out the door.

"My," Michael cooed, "So uptight aren't we?"

"Just what was that crack about Madeline being barely covered!" screamed Jack.

"Oh, Jackie, don't get fussy with me, let me make you a Bloody Mary," and with that he swished off to the bar.

# Chapter 28

At Madeline's they found nothing but hungry dogs.

"I can't believe this!" Joe roared, "the damn place isn't even locked!"

David looked in the refrigerator and found a can of dog food and fed the dogs, who were very happy to have the company. "Poor things." he commented.

"Yeah, right. People should have it so good." grumbled Joe.

"Joe, is there something going on between you and Madeline Fox that I don't know about? You seem, out of the ordinary, agitated."

"This shit is really getting to me, David. This son of a bitch must be laughing his ass off! Now, Madeline! We've got to find her alive, David!"

"We will, Joe." he said without much confidence.

"Lets get back over to the party scene and walk the grid. Call the CS techs right away and lets rope off the area. We've got to find something!"

They all arrived back there at the same time and started their duties. They dusted Madeline's car for prints, pried open the trunk, looking for her body, and went back and forth from the door of the house to her car door. Finally they found her car and house keys under the car lodged against the front drivers wheel.

"Shit! He took her from behind just before she got into her car!" screamed Joe. "Why the hell did she drive anyway? She's just a few houses away from this place!"

"Well, Joe, think about it. These "guys" have all white everything. She probably didn't want to track sand into this over decorated, over embellished, over rated palace! Heaven forbid you fuck up their stuff!"

"Shit, shit, shit!" Joe screamed.

# Chapter 29

"I am so cold I can hardly think. I've got to think! How will he kill me? He tore the other women to shreds! He said he'd be easy on me. If he unties me, what do I need to do to overtake him? Knee to the groin? No, wait! My shoes! Thank God I'd chosen these stupid 3" rhinestone encrusted, uncomfortable, ridiculous things! They were a weapon! I just needed to get untied, and I'd impale him with one of them! But, would he untie me, or would he just kill me here?"

I started to work the ropes on my wrists. Weird knot. The rope felt rough against my wrists. Forget the pain! I needed to work free of the ropes. I can do this! And I went to work. At the same time, I decided I'd wiggle my feet, hoping the rope around my ankles would loosen. Wow, this was generating heat for my body! Well, at least I wouldn't freeze to death!

I could feel the blood running down my hands and my feet, but kept working the ropes. I had to get them loose. My good friend, Linda, who is Deputy Sheriff for Columbia, Mo, once said to me "but us redheads are stubborn, stable women, who are not mowed down by the likes of most men! Rise above it, my friend and look forward to the New Year with the determination that this will indeed be your year to find great happiness, wealth and a man who adores you, who is truly worthy of you!!" God Bless Linda! I needed to keep those words in my mind and my heart.

My thoughts raced. Tony, my God, I would never have suspected Tony! I didn't know women laughed at him and called him a mama's boy. Mama Maria was truly controlling, but Tony is a hard worker and a very attractive man. Did he ask them out and get turned down? And what's this about me spoiling myself? That's sick! Sex is a natural function! It's socially accepted, unlike murder, and does positive things for our bodies. Like relieve stress, so we don't murder people! Man, what a sicko. Wait a minute, how does he know I "fucked" the cop? Has he been spying on me? What a creep!

# Chapter 30

Joe was frantic. Madeline! We have to find her, he thought. I don't know what I'll do if... his thoughts were interrupted just then by Christensen.

"Joe this is going nowhere. This guy just doesn't make mistakes! We need to think of where he might have taken her, and how. We need a guest list, who drove and who walked, what time people left, and we need to find the people who would have noticed Madeline leaving, since these guys obviously didn't pay attention!"

"You're right, David. I'm just not thinking clearly."

"Joe, what's going on with you and Madeline? I thought you were a confirmed bachelor."

"Shut up, Christensen!" and stormed back into the house for some answers.

Jack and Michael were downing Bloody Mary's like there was no tomorrow.

"Listen guys, I need some answers and I need you both sober. Who would have seen Madeline leave, and know if anyone else left at the same time? We also need a guest list and a list of any hired help you might have had."

"Well," Michael sprung into action, "We always hire from Buffy Butlers for serving and Creative Caterers usually does our food. The liquor is delivered by Booze Busters, but they would have come and gone long before the party. We also use the local florist Bloomin' Wacky, but they would also come long before the party."

"Any drugs, guys?" asked Joe.

Jack jumped up from his chaise in anger, and screamed, "we don't do drugs, officer!"

"OK, OK, settle down Jack. I'm not accusing you, but what about any of your guests?"

"Look, we may get a little pie-eyed, but we don't hang with that crowd." Jack snorted.

# Chapter 31

"I think our best bet is Buffy Butlers," Joe said as they pulled away from the mansion. "Hopefully, those guys weren't drinking and can remember something. Let's head down there."

"OK." from David.

Buffy Butlers also provided Sexy Servers, depending on what your fancy was. As they pulled up in the squad car and entered the building, it was obvious they made some people very uncomfortable.

Joe walked up to the receptionist, or what ever she was, and asked to see the manager. She squirmed in her little chair and asked what type of business they were conducting.

At this point Joe pulled out his badge and stuck it in her face. She immediately punched some buttons on her phone and in a hushed voice said, "Mr. Slick, there are some police officers here to see you." she looked up sheepishly at Joe.

Just then a door burst open and Mr. Slick appeared.

"What can I do for you gentlemen?" he inquired.

"Let's go into your office," Joe ordered.

They got the list of "Buffy Butlers" that worked last nights party, along with their addresses and left.

"Man, it takes all kinds," growled Christensen.

"Yeah." was all he got out of Joe.

# Chapter 32

"You realize, Joe, that this was how the first vic was abducted. Leaving a party on the beach."

"If we don't find her alive, David, I don't know what I'll do."

"OK, Joe, just what the hell is going on between you two?"

"Mind your own God damned business, Christensen!"

"Okay, let's talk to the first Buffy Butler on our list." Christensen muttered.

There were a dozen on the list, holy cow, Joe thought! How many butlers does it take to splash some wine into a glass!

He just ached for her. That was the sum and total of it. She was by far the most incredible woman he had ever known! He wanted to explode with frustration! If anything happened to her…if he couldn't protect her…good God! What was he to do? She was so sweet, so soft, so incredible! Shit, shit, shit, he thought! He had never been this frustrated!

He needed to think! He needed to loose the emotional connection. It was clouding his mind. He needed to think clearly or he'd loose her forever!

The first victim was killed on the beach, the second on the beach, the third on the beach! If he was acting true to form, she was near here somewhere! Shit, would they find her body in the morning! No way! She had to be alive!

OK, he thought, there had to be hiding places on the beach. Maybe he took her to his home. They were combing the beach now and had been for several hours. For some reason he didn't kill her right away like the others. He had her hid somewhere. Was she conscious? Was she gagged and tied up? Had he beat her, or raped her? We know he didn't do that to the other victims, but was she special in some way? He knew then he had never felt that way about any other case he had worked on. Yeah, right, he thought, you never fell in love with the others either!

Shit, shit, shit!

# Chapter 33

I knew I was bloody, I could feel and smell it. The ropes were finally loose, thank God! The only underwear I had on were those high cut silk panties that amounted to nothing! If I made it out of here alive, I made a promise to buy only cotton or flannel undies from here on out! No more sexy, tiny, lacey, pieces of shit!

I was so frustrated!

Just then the door burst open and Tony appeared. He had his arms full of something.

He approached me saying, "Mia, I bring candles, your favorite wine, and a supper for just the two of us."

"I be so in love with you for so long, I want wonderful evening with you before you die. I even make love to you, so you know what is right."

"Oh, Tony," I replied, "I have always been so attracted to you, too, and wondered why you never asked me for a date!"

"Mia, Fox, I be so afraid you turn me down!"

"Oh, no, Tony! You are so handsome! I'm sorry to ask this of you, Tony, but could you loosen the ropes, please? I feel like I'm bleeding because of their tightness."

"Oh, Mia, let me assist you! Oh, my, I need to cleanse you!"

"Oh, Tony, why have we not ended up together? I wish I'd have known of your interest in me!" I lied.

"Mia, we get everything settled tonight!"

He removed the ropes, and bathed my hands and ankles. Then he lit the candles, laid out a blanket, spread the food and wine in a lavish setting, and turned to me.

"Mia, I so in love with you. Let me hold and kiss you, then we eat. After we eat, we seal our love for each other, and you understand where you make mistake.

I knew I needed to go along with him to bide my time. So I did. I would act like I was totally in love with him, and would do anything he asked.

The food smelled wonderful and I knew I needed my strength. The wine would keep me calm, but I'd have to be careful as it had been a long time since I had eaten anything. I didn't want it to go straight to my head. Well, there's a thought, maybe if I don't escape him my death would be easier if I was drunk.

Tony handed me a large goblet filled to the brim of my favorite Pinot. He looked at me with love in his eyes and clinked his glass to mine. "To us!" he toasted.

We started with a Pasta and Fagiola Soup, followed by Manicotti ala Forno.

"Oh, Tony, the Manicotti is exquisite! The Ricotta and Mozzarella cheeses make it so creamy."

"Only the best for you, Mia."

I didn't realize I was so hungry until I started to eat. We finished with a Tiramisu that was moist and creamy, just the way it should be. Tony poured us more wine.

What now, I thought.

"Gee, all we need is a fireplace," I blurted out. I was definitely nervous.

"Mia, let me clean up then, well you know, we make good love so you know right from wrong."

OK, I thought, this is when I'll need to be ready to make my move.

# Chapter 34

Finally, in the interview with Buffy Butler #8, he said he noticed the restaurant guy leave just about the same time she did.

"You mean Tony?"

"Yeah, that's the dude. Eat there sometimes, pretty good joint."

"Do you think we should interview the rest, Joe?"

"Put a man on it, but the rest of us will go to Tony's now!" he screamed.

It only took a few minutes to get there. They rang the bell, but no answer. Joe turned the knob and the door opened easily.

"Shit, doesn't anybody around here lock their doors!"

They went in calling out Tony's name, but got no response.

"Call the restaurant and see if he's there." Joe ordered.

"Not there."

Where, he thought, where could he have taken her? "Christensen, check with the officer that's doing the rest of the interviews, see if he's learned anything else."

"He's on number eleven. Nothing." from a worried Christensen.

"Let's head back out." Joe croaked.

# Chapter 35

Tony finished his clean up and put everything back into the wicker basket. He had opened the second bottle of wine and again refilled our glasses. Maybe I could get him drunk, I thought.

He leaned over and kissed my mouth. I responded as best I could, but was repulsed.

"Oh, Mia, you taste so sweet." he gushed.

"Oh, Tony, you are the best kisser I've ever known." I fibbed. "Why don't you give us a second chance so we can be together forever? If you kill me, it's over!"

"Mia, you spoil yourself. I no want you for my wife now."

"But, Tony, if you love me you can forgive me!"

"No forgive. Would never forget you spoil youself for me."

"Then why don't you just kill me now?" I said angrily.

"I need to show you right love."

With that he pushed me onto my back with force. My wine glass smashed onto the concrete and left me with a jagged goblet in my grasp. I slammed it into his face and heard him howl. I took my foot and shoved it directly into his groin. All 3" of spike heel. He screamed and fell backwards swearing loudly in Italian.

I grabbed the shoes from my feet, hiked my dress up to my waist and flew from the lighthouse into the night. I knew he'd be after me so I headed for the nearest cover I could find. This would be the boathouse that belonged to the Oxford's. I lifted the cover of the speed boat and climbed in, pulling the cover back down. I curled into a tight little ball and listened for any noise.

I could feel glass fragments in my hand. I knew I was bleeding, and hoped I hadn't left a trail of blood to my hiding place. But, it was dark and would be harder to spot any drips of blood in the sand, I hoped.

# Chapter 36

"Get the spot lights!" screamed Joe. "That old abandoned lighthouse is up ahead!"

They burst into the old lighthouse and saw the basket filled with the remains of dinner, the two empty wine bottles, a blanket, candles still burning and glass shards. Then they saw the blood.

"Call the CS Techs, now! Get those lights into the sand and look for a trail of blood! Let's go!"

David knew Joe was totally out of control. He'd never seen him like this. Just what the hell was going on, he thought.

Joe actually found himself praying silently that it wasn't Madeline's blood they were tracking. He felt like he would have a nervous breakdown if they didn't find her alive. Oh, my God, what would he do!

Right then he promised God that he would never do another wrong thing in his whole life, never swear, always go to Mass and join the Priesthood if only he could find Madeline alive.

# Chapter 37

I could hear someone scurring through the sand. I didn't move a muscle, and barely let myself breathe. The doors to the boathouse were yanked open. The light of the moon spilled in, then the doors slammed shut.

Whew, I thought. He wasn't smart enough to check the boat!

I stayed very still and continued to listen. I thought I heard some shouting from somewhere. But, I stayed in my little hiding place.

There were windows in the little boathouse and I caught the reflection of flashlights or lanterns through the canvas that covered the boat.

My heart leapt. Could it be Joe? I prayed with all my heart that it was!

Again the doors burst open. But this time someone ripped the tarp off the boat. I screamed, thinking it was Tony, but was surrounded by cops!

"Madeline!" Joe screamed and ran to lift me from the boat.

He held me in his arms and I could feel his body shaking. I was enveloped in the warmth. I took deep breaths of his smell. He took off his jacket and put it on me.

"Get the hell out of here and find the bastard!" he screamed.

"It was Tony, Joe!"

"We know, baby. We'll find him. There were two sets of blood trails. Did you wound him?"

"Yes, with a broken wine glass."

He then yelled at Christensen to follow the other trail of blood.

"I'm taking you to my place."

"Joe, Tony told me the reason he needed to kill me was because 'I fucked the cop,' and ruined myself."

"OK, we won't go to my place. I'll take you somewhere safe until we find him."

Joe gathered me in his arms and we headed to the squad car. The heat was blowing full blast and I shivered violently. He looked at me with such concern, I said, "It's OK, Joe, it feels so good."

He went to the drivers door, yanked it open and got in.

He drove downtown to the Residence Inn and parked. "You're coming in with me. I'm not letting you out of my sight." he growled.

We checked in and drove to the suite he rented. He built a roaring fire and wrapped me in a blanket as I sat on the corner of the sofa. He called and checked with Christensen about their progress, and told him where we were. He ordered a squad car to be outside the door until Tony was found.

"I'll be right back." he said.

I looked at him with fear in my eyes.

"You'll be fine, I promise. I won't be gone long."

I did feel safe, and with the warmth of the fire and the blanket, I felt myself dozing off. I'm not sure how much time had gone by, but the next thing I knew the door to the suite was opening. I jerked upright afraid it was Tony, but it was Joe. I let out a sigh of relief.

He had several packages under his arms. "Nice dress, but put these on." he said, and held out a pair of pink sweats and a pair of fluffy slippers. Then he unbagged several bottles of wine and bourbon, chunks of cheese and a can of coffee.

"I guess we're spending the night." I commented.

"The night or however long we have to until Tony is found."

"Look, I'd really like to take a shower, if you don't mind. I feel kind of gritty. What else have you in those bags?" I asked. "You'll see." was all he said.

# Chapter 38

I let the hot water pour over me until the bathroom was so full of steam you could see nothing. I scrubbed my body and my hair until I was almost raw, then turned off the taps.

The towels were rough and thick, and I rubbed my skin with their roughness. I put on the soft sweats. Wow, he did good, I thought. These were made of a very soft cotton velvet that felt wonderful against my skin. How did he know my size, I wondered.

I towel dried my hair, brushed my teeth, and felt somewhat back to normal again.

When I exited the bath, I found him pulling the cork out of one of the bottles of wine.

"Do you mind if I have a bourbon?" I asked. "I've had a little too much wine already tonight."

"No problem," he said. "Come here and let me see those wrists and ankles."

He opened yet another bag and pulled out salve and gauze bandages. Very gently he applied the ointment, and wrapped lovingly. "Can't have you getting infection."

We sat in front of the fire, his arm around me, sipping our bourbon. Part of me wanted to cry from relief, but I didn't want him to think of me as a cry baby. It felt so good to be with him. He had so much strength, and I felt so protected.

"Have you found him yet?" I asked.

"Not yet, but we will. Do you want to talk about what happened, or would you rather wait until morning?"

"Morning, please Joe. But, my girls!"

"Already taken care of, don't worry. They've been fed and watered. They're fine.

By the way, don't you lock your door?"

"Well," I said.

"Right," he said.

He held her and thanked God she was safe with him.

# Chapter 39

"Are you hungry?"

"No," I replied, "Tony had quite a lavish 'Last Supper' for us."

"I saw the basket of remains."

We sat there for a long time watching the fire and holding each other.

"Let's go to bed." I said.

"I thought you'd never ask." he smiled.

Again, he picked me up in his arms and carried me to the bed. I slid my clothes from my body and heard him groan. He tore his clothing off and I could see that he was rock hard. He entered me with a force that took my breath away. He caressed my breasts and kissed them softly. He was thrusting in and out of me so skillfully that I thought I'd loose my mind. Then I exploded in a violent orgasm that just kept going. When I thought mine would never end, he exploded inside of me, letting out a groan of relief. He was by far the best lover I'd ever had.

I fell asleep in his arms against his warm body.

He never let go of her all night. He was almost afraid to go to sleep. He could have wept with relief when they found her. He'd make sure nothing ever happened to her again! He'd protect her with his own life if he had to. He had never known such an incredible woman. And she was a total woman.

After all she'd been through for the last few days, she still had it together. The bruises and torn flesh on her wrists and ankles told him she had been bound. Laying on that cold concrete floor in that wisp of a dress, it's a wonder she didn't die of exposure! God was certainly looking after her! Thank God! he thought.

He tried to relax and go to sleep. Her breathing was solid and even. She looked like an angel in her sleep. He kissed her hair and held her close. Finally total exhaustion took over and he fell sound asleep.

# Chapter 40

They woke around ten, obviously both exhausted from the ordeal. Man, she even looks good in the morning, Joe thought.

She smiled sweetly up at him and he kissed her.

"Hungry?" he asked.

"Starved!" I said.

"OK, I'll start the coffee and bacon, you get the shower first."

"It's a deal." I replied.

When I stepped from the shower I could smell the coffee and bacon. I dressed quickly in the pretty cotton sweats Joe had brought for me, and headed for the kitchen.

"Have you heard anything yet?" I asked.

"They still haven't found him." Joe said disgustedly.

"Oh, my."

"We will, baby, don't you worry. You're safe here with me."

He handed me a steaming mug of coffee.

"Any cream?" I asked.

"Well, not knowing how you took your coffee, I did buy half and half!"

"Wonderful!" I said. "You're a special man, Joe."

"I take that as the utmost compliment." He added the cream to my coffee, continued to fry the bacon, and started breaking eggs into a bowl.

"What can I do?" I asked.

"Just sit there and look beautiful." he smiled. "Scrambled OK?"

"Perfect," I replied.

He whipped the eggs, added cheese and a little milk, and dumped all of it into the hot skillet.

"You'll make someone a great wife!" I teased.

"I hope so." he laughed.

He popped toast into the toaster, poured us both orange juice, and we sat down to eat.

"This is wonderful! Thank you, Joe."

"My pleasure."

After breakfast, I insisted I clean up while he took his shower, and a worried look crossed his face.

"Don't open the door to anyone and don't go outside for any reason." he said sternly.

"OK, Joe. Don't worry. Now go clean yourself up!" I teased.

Reluctantly he left the room. He would hurry. He hated it when she was out of his sight. They still hadn't found the murdering bastard and it made him nervous. He'd love to get his hands on the sicko. He'd tear him from limb to limb, thought Joe. Give him a little taste of his own medicine! Jesus, he feeds them and then murders them! He'd like to feed him all right, with one of his own body parts.

When he emerged from the bath, he saw she had a fire going and was curled up at the end of the sofa with a cup of coffee.

"Can I get you another cup, Joe?" I asked.

"No thank you."

We laid around all day watching the fire, and movies, and making love in front of the fireplace.

Around four I declared, "it's cocktail hour!"

So I poured the wine and we snuggled in front of the fire.

"Let's order Chinese!"

"How do you keep that incredible figure the way you eat?" Joe laughed.

"Lot's of sex!"

"Yeah, right."

Before he called in the order, Joe checked in with David. Not yet, was all he got. Where was the bastard? What if he kills again?

"OK, what will it be?" he asked.

"Garlic chicken, please!"

"Oh, boy, I'd better get something garlic too, or I won't be able to stand to kiss you!"

I slapped him playfully on the arm, and laughed.

It was so good to hear her laugh. He thought he might never hear that sound again.

He had to stop thinking like this, she's safe. He placed the order and put his arms around her again.

"I could get used to this." I said.

He felt his heart swoon.

"Joe, lets go ahead and talk about what you need to know while we wait for our delivery."

"You sure you're ready?"

"Yes, I'd kind of like to get it over with."

"Just go through slowly what happened." he said gently.

"I had been out on appointments all day with potentially new clients. When I got home there was the invitation to Michael and David's in the door. Well, they always throw the best parties, so of course I was going. I decided to drive the short distance, because I didn't want to track in sand. Not long after I arrived, I saw Tony across the room, I waived, but he just seemed to stare in my direction. I never really saw him the rest of the evening, but I was talking to people I knew and some I just met." My thoughts went back to Gabrielle and Mack, and I chuckled.

"What?" Joe asked.

"Oh, nothing, another story. I still didn't see Tony when I said good-bye to my hosts, so I don't know if he was still inside the house or hiding outside waiting for me. As I approached my car I heard a noise behind me, he grabbed me and shoved this horrible smelling rag over my nose and mouth. That's the last thing I remember until I came to in the light house."

"Thank God you drove. That's the only way we knew you were missing, otherwise he could have killed you before anybody even missed you." he said with a shudder.

"Oh, and the rag, was doused in Chloroform. It knocks you out temporarily. We found your keys lodged under the front wheel and figured you were grabbed from behind. Did he, did he touch you, Madeline?"

"No, but that was his plan. He said I spoiled myself with you, and he needed to show me the difference between right and wrong love. Then he shoved me backwards so hard my wine glass shattered on the floor. I slammed it into his face and when he drew backwards, I nailed him with my 3" stiletto in the groin!"

"Oh, man, you hurt him bad! It's a miracle you got out of there alive!"

There was a knock on the door. Joe jumped up and pulled the gun from the waist of his jeans.

"Whose there?" he asked as he peered through the peep hole.

"Delivery! I have Chinese food for Fredosa!"

Joe punched in a number into the cell phone. "Get up here and see if this guy's for real, rookie!" Then he punched in another number, "Christensen! Get me an experienced cop out here, even if you have to do it yourself!"

"He checks out Commander Fredosa," the rookie said sheepishly.

Joe yanked open the door, shoved a bill into the delivery guy's hand, grabbed the bag, and slammed the door shut twisting the locks. He muttered something under his breath then came back to sit down beside me.

"You OK?" I asked.

"I will be." he grumbled.

We ate takeout Chinese food from the little cartons using chop sticks, and sharing with each other. I refilled our wine glasses, and I could see Joe start to relax again. I kind of felt sorry for that young rookie cop, but I did feel safer now knowing someone had replaced him. I wondered if it was Detective Christensen.

# Chapter 41

He would find the whore! And this time no Mr. Nice Guy. He'd kill her on the spot! She'd hurt him, bad, and now she'd pay.

As he searched the beach for her he came upon a couple making love in the sand.

This put him over the edge of fury. He slammed the boys head into the girls face, bones crunched and popped, and the blood flew.

Now he was completely out of control. She'd made a fool of him, making him believe she loved him. He couldn't think of enough bad things to do to her when he found her. Oh, and he would find her, if it was the last thing he ever did.

He ducked behind a yacht as he heard voices. Cops. Fuck. Their lanterns were lighting up everything. He wondered if he'd left a trail of blood to his hiding place.

"Over here! Quick!" an officer shouted.

He needed to move. They didn't seem to be looking for a trail, the dumb asses, but were totally engrossed in trying to decide if the couple were still alive. Good, he could make his break!

"Better call Christensen. Let him call Fredosa. Jesus, we've got to stop him! He can't be far, this is very fresh. You stay here Briggs until Christensen arrives. Everybody else, let's go! Briggs, call an ambulance and the CS Techs right after Christensen."

"I'll be there as soon as I get a replacement." Christensen responded.

He tried Lutinent Zimpfer again and got him this time. Will, get over here to the Residence Inn and guard suite 23. We've got Fredosa and Madeline in there. He's killed again!" Christensen punched in another number, "This ain't right, he's done it again."

"Shit, shit, shit! Call me as soon as you've got details!" Fredosa snapped the phone shut.

"What's all the yelling about, Joe?" I asked as I came out of the bathroom.

"Oh God no! He's killed again?" I started to shake, violently.

Joe raced across the room to me pulling me in to his arms.

"Let me do the worrying, baby. We'll get him soon." He held her tightly and thought they could only pray that they got him soon.

## Chapter 42

When Christensen got there the ambulance and the CS Techs had already arrived.

"Move!" he said to someone. "Have the bodies been touched?"

"Of course not Detective, I've guarded them until you arrived." the officer said.

"Good, now let me take a look. Give me that light!" he just stared in disbelief. "OK, meds, separate them."

Their heads looked like a war zone. The boy's penis was still stuck in the girl! There were bone fracture splinters and teeth stuck in the blood. So much blood.

"OK, take them away." Christensen said quietly. "Tech's, call me as soon as you have something." and walked slowly back to his car.

He didn't relish seeing his boss, but headed to the hotel.

"What the hell is happening out there, David!" he screamed.

"Joe, let's try to stay calm and clear headed. It was a couple of kids making out on the beach. He rammed their heads together so hard, they died instantly. Never knew what hit them."

I started to cry. Joe came over and put my head on his shoulder. "Shhhh, baby. It'll be OK. What's happening out there now David?"

"Griggs left one officer to guard the kids and took off with the rest of his men. It was obvious they came upon the kids very soon after it happened, so I believe we're closing in on him."

"Better be." Joe said sternly.

"Joe, I need to have my babies here with me." I cried.

"David, go get them, don't forget food and dog dishes. Madeline, do you need him to bring anything else for you?"

"Not really, I'm fine."

"You still have her keys David?"

"Yeah. I'll be right back."

## Chapter 43

They searched all night with no luck. He certainly was crafty. Hopefully they can find him in the daylight.

Christensen looked like shit when he entered the station. "Give me an update, Griggs."

"We searched all night and couldn't find him. I hope we have better luck in the daylight. I'm putting my team together now. My other men are exhausted and I need fresh eyes. We still have a watch on the restaurant and his house, but he'd be stupid if he showed up there."

"Just keep me posted." Christensen sighed. When will this all end, he thought. He was exhausted. Joe was breathing down his neck, hell, he's in love with her, he thought. It was crystal clear in his eyes and body language. No wonder he'd been such an ass hole to work with. He'd never seen him like this before. Well, she'd be one hell of a catch, that's for sure! Why does it seem like women always get in the way of good judgment? he thought with a little jealousy.

Those dogs had been nearly hysterical to see her. Very well behaved, he thought. Well, I suppose everything in her life was in order. And she didn't even request all that fussy stuff women usually want. Maybe it was because she was beautiful without all that shit they plaster on the faces. She was tan, had the most perfectly white teeth he'd ever seen, and just glowed. Even after what had happened to her she looked good. Fuck! I'll never forget the morning I showed up at her house unexpected, he thought. She was all put together and dewy. Whatever! He was through with women!

He pulled out a map and scanned the beach area, trying to figure out where the bastard was. He swore under his breath and hunkered down.

He drew a highlighter over the path that they knew he had taken, but that of course didn't mean he'd go in a straight line. He needed to know what buildings and boathouses were stationed where. He pulled another drawing and started to compare.

# Chapter 44

Man, these guys are idiots, he thought for the hundredth time. He had to figure out where they'd hidden her. Even those mutts weren't barking, so they must have moved them all together.

Well, after he killed her, he'd have to kill himself, something he hadn't planned on. Otherwise Mama Maria would do it for him. Fuck, maybe he'd kill her instead and be free of the old bat. He'd have to leave town and hide in some Caribbean island. Oh well, it could be worse. At least the women over there would know none of his past! He'd be treated like he should be!

To think of it, she had to be with the cop that fucked her! Christ, why hadn't he thought of this before? He rented a place somewhere on the beach, he thought, but didn't know for sure where. Wait a minute! The Henderson Cottage! That had to be it. Old man Henderson croaked in the Spring, and the widow moved somewhere to be with a son, or was it a daughter? Who cared! That's where they were! Bingo! Too bad the cops weren't as smart as he was!

He started working his way toward the cottage. He needed to be careful in case they were watching the place. He wasn't worried. He had outsmarted them time after time so far! He was careful to stay away from the areas lit by the street lamps. He ducked in and out of boathouses and docks until he reached the Henderson Cottage.

No lights were on, they were probably fucking again! What a whore! Maybe I'll kill her then fuck her, he thought. Yeah, that's what he'd do, that way she couldn't ram him in the groin with her fucking shoe again. Jesus, he thought, can I even get it up after what she'd done to me? This thought infuriated him. The bitch could have ruined me! Oh, the things I'll do to her, he planned.

The doors were locked. He snuck around to where he knew the bedroom should be, but it was so dark he couldn't see a thing. Right now he wished he'd grabbed the flashlight before he took off after her, but he was in so much pain he hadn't thought about it. Should he break a window?

Maybe he'd hide in the boathouse, wait and watch until he saw movement. Good idea, that will give me time to think of other places to look, he thought.

# Chapter 45

I was having so much fun playing with my girls! Joe liked them too, which was definitely a point for his side. He had had Detective Christensen go by the supermarket and pick us up a list of groceries we had made out for him, and tonight Joe was making one of the things he enjoyed making the most, spaghetti!

I went into the kitchen to help him with the salad. He looked the most peaceful and relaxed I'd ever seen him. He was pampering his sauce, and I slid my arms around his waste and kissed the side of his neck, he shivered. Big bad cop wasn't so bad after all, I thought.

"Smells wonderful," I nudged his ear.

"Shit, Madeline, you are driving me crazy!"

"OK, I'll start the salad."

I rinsed lettuce, chopped onion, celery, green, red and yellow pepper, cleaned fresh mushrooms, and added a little carrot.

I could smell the garlic bread in the oven, and noticed Joe was opening two bottles of red wine. He had a pot of boiling water going for the pasta.

What a man, I thought. Just being with him was so easy, so comfortable. Actually, it was a little scary how good we were together. I wonder how he really feels about me, I thought. Is he just doing his job, along with a little bonus of fucking me, or did he have true feelings for me? I guess I'll find out when all of this is over, I thought.

I set the little table for us, then fed my girls. Joe was draining the pasta, I put the salad on the table and he heaped our plates for us. I poured the wine, and we sat down.

It's kind of like a fairy tale world, I thought. No bills to pay, no phone calls to return, no house to clean. Wait a minute, I thought! I've got two new clients! I need to be making notes and planning for them! How the hell could I have forgotten! This was not like me, my reputation was at stake, this is my livelihood!

"Joe, is there anything to write on?" I asked.

"Why?" he asked while twirling his spaghetti onto the spoon.

"Well, I'm mortified that I just remembered I have two new clients! I need to make notes, and I really need to get back to my place to do research."

"OK, let's start with mortified. After all you've been through, you're surprised that you forgot? And, secondly, you are not going back to your place until he is found! So, get that through your stubborn red head right now. And, if you pull anything on me you'll get yourself killed for sure this time."

"Wow," I said. "I think I've just been knocked down a notch."

"Yeah, that would be the case," he smiled.

"The spaghetti sauce is to die for, Joe."

"Well, let's not go that far, and let's not talk about dying!"

"You're right, again. But, it is very wonderful!"

"Thank you, Ms. Fox."

After dinner and we cleaned up, we took the second bottle of wine and our glasses and went to sit in front of the fire.

Just then Joe's cell phone rang. "Joe." he responded.

"No good news, that's for sure." David said.

"What now, David?"

"We've got men on his place, the restaurant, your place and Madeline's. He's a sneaky bastard. Again it's dark. You know it's harder to find him then. He's probably hiding in some boathouse, and we're not finding him."

"Have you researched a map of the area?"

"Done. But how the hell do we know where he'll go? He's got to be looking for her, she humiliated him and wounded him! Christ, he's on a rampage, and he's got us looking like idiots!"

"Well, you've certainly got that right! Listen David, could you get some pens, legal pads and note cards over here first thing in the morning?"

"What for?"

"Never mind! Just do it! And call me when you have anything." with out waiting for a response, he hung up.

"Thank you, Joe!" I said relieved.

"No problem."

But he looked upset again. Man, does this guy have mood swings, or what! I leaned onto him and he put his arms around me. The girls were curled up in front of the fire. Wow, this is a Norman Rockwell painting, I thought.

He had such a sexy smell. It wasn't soap or cologne, or even deodorant. It was just his natural fragrance. It almost drove me wild with lustful thoughts! He was always so immaculate. His clothing was impeccable. Everything always matched. He never had a hair out of place. He was driving me wild, I thought! I don't know if I'm ready for this, or even if I want it!

The wine was going to my head, a little. I started to kiss his ear, then his neck. He turned and kissed me full on my lips, and I let out a sigh. His kisses became more intense, and I felt such a need for him. We held each other with such deep feelings, I really felt like we were so good together. Actually, for the first time in nine years, I might possibly love again. We had such a connection, both physically and mentally. But, did I dare? Do I just throw caution to the wind?

He was obviously thinking similar things, as he looked at me in a funny way.

"Madeline, I'm not sure how to say this but, I think I'm in love with you."

Tears sprang to my eyes, and he put his index finger gently over my lips.

That night we made the most perfect, tender love. I think right then and there I knew I was in love with him too.

# Chapter 46

We woke pretty much all in a ball, between Joe, myself, Topaz and Onyx. Man, life is good, I thought.

Suddenly I could hear a pounding on the door to the suite. "Joe!" I exclaimed. "There's someone at the door!" the dogs started barking and Joe untangled himself from me, grabbed a robe and said, "it's probably Christensen with your stuff." and headed out of the bedroom.

I listened, just to be sure, and it was Detective Christensen, and Joe invited him in for coffee, to go over things.

He stuck his head in the bedroom door and said, "It's David, we're going to go over some things, I'll make coffee, why don't you hit the shower and then join us?"

"OK, Joe," I said.

"I'll feed and water the girls, so take your time."

"You're wonderful, thank you."

He smiled, and shut the door. He started the coffee, then walked the dogs, and when he got back, David had poured two steaming mugs and started a fire. Joe put the dog food on the floor in the corner, got them fresh water and thanked David as he handed him a mug.

"Let's sit by the fire," said David.

"OK, David, what's next?"

"I gotta be honest with you, Joe, this guy has got us by the balls! Do you have any suggestions?"

At that moment, Madeline appeared from the bedroom. "Hello, Detective Christensen! How are you doing today? Don't get up Joe, I'll get my own coffee. May I join you, or is this a private conversation?"

## Chapter 47

God he was horny. All this thought about Madeline, the whore. He knew he'd fuck her either before or after he killed her. His dick was so hard thinking about her in her whore dress! What a God damned body! Fuck me! he thought. At least she didn't mame my damned dick!

They didn't show up in the light of day so he knew they weren't at the cops place, but where? Oh, piss, he thought! Of course they wouldn't go to his or her place because they'd know that would be the first place he'd check! They had to be at a hotel or a motel! Think! Where would a cop hold her up? Probably some cheap motel, he thought. Heaven forbid the Department spring for a Holiday Inn! He'd grab a phone book and start his research! God, he was good! Brilliant! However, he had this problem of his erection. He'd just have to jack off for now. Then he'd really be ready for the whore, and he could fuck her to death! He started to rub himself with her image in his mind.

After a few minutes, he let out a groan, and realized, with a laugh, he had just christened the cops boat! He wanted to roar with laughter, but had to be careful because he didn't know if the cops were close by.

He needed to find a pay phone somewhere and steal the phone book. He was not familiar with all the local hotels and motels. Fuck, how the hell is he going to figure out which one they're in! Or they might have a hiding place where they took people they were trying to protect! He was furious. He had to find the cops that were looking for him and follow them. Surely they'd have to report back to wherever they're holed up. OK, that's it!

Shit, he muttered as he ducked from the window of the boathouse. He had seen someone up by the cops house! God, he hoped they hadn't seen him! Now was his chance! He'd follow whoever he just saw and he'd lead him to her.

He snuck from the boathouse and ran to the first nearest hiding spot, then kept inching his way toward the house, checking every direction for anybody else that could spot him.

## Chapter 48

"He's probably lurking around Madeline's or my place. I think you just need to keep going back and checking our places." Joe was saying. "He really has no where to go. He knows better than to chance going to his place or the restaurant. The guy's crafty. He's gotta find Madeline, and he'll do whatever it takes to do so. Have your men watch their backs."

"All right, Joe, I'll head back over and take another look around your place. Then I'll go by Madeline's. I'll report back to you later."

"Bye, Detective," turning to Joe I said, "I'm really getting cabin fever!"

"Too bad, you can't go anywhere."

"Gee, you don't have to get ugly about it." I grumbled.

I walked to the little desk and sat down with my pad and started to make some notes on my ideas for Mrs. Thoroughgood's gourmet kitchen. In the early days this New England house was a single room (half-house) with a chimney on the side. Then the size was doubled by repeating the original room on the other side of the chimney. In this way the chimney became the central feature of the house and the fireplace could be opened in each room, creating the Cape Cod style.

This particular chimney effect opened into the kitchen and the cocktail parlour. According to the Chef it was very common for guests to congregate in the large kitchen. There was a large pantry off the back of the kitchen, where she would layout a design that would include a meat storage locker. There would need to be a bin for fresh fruit and vegetables, and then the area for hanging and drying.

As for the kitchen itself, it needed some new equipment and some needed to be larger than what she currently had. It would all be stainless steel. At one end there was a huge oak table with very ornate legs of an early English design. That would stay, the floor was ceramic and I wanted a large area rug for under the table. A dark one to contrast the white tile floor. The kitchen is extremely well lit, however I wanted softer lighting near the table to make it less harsh. I think I will also add a Bakers Rack to the area to hold a lamp for soft lighting.

Remembering just then, I looked up and said to Joe, "I need to contact Mrs. Hawthorne today. I am supposed to receive her shipment tomorrow, and I need to call Ellen White at Needless Treasures to stop the delivery.

"I'll have it taken care of, Madeline."

"Joe what's the matter?"

"What's the matter? What's the matter! They can't find him, that's what's the matter! He's smarter than he looks."

"Would you like me to fix us a cocktail?"

"No, you go ahead though, I need to stay focused."

I went to the little bar and splashed some bourbon over ice, and added a little Diet Coke.

I sat back down at the little desk and started my notes for Mrs. Jefferson's dining room, and Mr. Jefferson's study. I will love doing the study, with it's wood covered walls and cove panels in the ceiling. I'll use warm rich colors, buttery soft leather upholstery, and the thickest carpets I can find to cover the beautiful hardwood floors under his desk and in the seating area. The Doctor had plenty of books, with one whole wall section of custom shelves, I just needed to rearrange them and add a few interesting pieces that I'm sure I'll find at Needful Treasures.

Now for the dining room. Victorian, my favorite! First we'll paint the walls a full bodied amethyst, then find a rug for under the table done in jewel tones. The table, hutch and server will be a rich, heavy oak, and the sparse lace curtains will be replaced by thick heavy fabrics. A custom centerpiece arrangement to tie in all the colors will be made for the dining room table.

"Joe, is there any way we could do take-out from that Mexican place just down the road a bit?"

"All you think about is food!"

"Of course it's not! I think about lot's of things."

# Chapter 49

Oh what luck, he thought! There's Christensen now, and he knew he reported directly to Fredosa. I'm brilliant, he again congratulated himself. He had to stay out of sight and run like hell. He hoped the bastard didn't drive to fast, because he had to make it on foot!

David checked again around the house and in the boathouse. Nothing, he'd head to Madeline's.

From there he decided to check around the restaurant. After finding nothing he went inside to speak with Mama Maria.

"I no see him! You leave him alone, he's a good boy! You no hurt him!"

"How do I know you're not hiding him?"

"I no hide! I no hide!"

Well, back to Joe with more bad news! He'd take his time getting there that's for sure. He didn't want to deal with this any sooner than he had to. He radioed Griggs hopeful of some good news. Nothing, they're still looking. Shit!

Up ahead he saw Joe crossing the street and pulled over to him.

"I hope you don't have more bad news for me."

Just then a shot rang out, Joe's head exploded, and he crashed to the ground.

Christensen was on the radio shouting for help and an ambulance while scanning the area the shot came from, then he flew from the car in a dead run with his weapon pulled. He saw the bastard up ahead pulled him into his sights, and fired. Tony hit the ground hard face down. David ran to him gun still pointed at him, but a few yards away he could see the entire backside of Tony's head was blown away. He checked for a pulse just in case and turned to run back to Joe.

The ambulance and several squad cars were screeching around the corner as he flew to Joe's motionless body. The whole side of his face was missing. He felt for a pulse as the medics arrived. "He's dead."

## Chapter 51

He slowly headed the squad car into the parking lot at the Residence Inn.

He knocked on the door calling out his name. He waited for her to look through the peep hole and open the door.

"Hi Detective! Please come in. Detective Christensen, you don't look so good. May I get you a drink?"

"You'd better sit down Miss Fox."

I grabbed my drink from the desk and went to the sofa.

"Joe's dead. Tony's dead."

"No!" I screamed. "You're wrong!"

"I'm not wrong. Tony killed Joe and I killed Tony. It's as simple as that. It's over."

I felt my whole body crumble, and I sobbed into my hands. Detective David Christensen crossed the room, sat down beside me and put his arm around me. I don't know how much time went by before there were no more tears in me and I hiccuped.

"Let me get you home, I have a lot of work to do. You're safe now."

I was numb. We gathered my things and my girls and headed to the squad car. The ambulance was just pulling away with the coroner's car right behind. Police officers were just standing there watching Joe's body being taken away, with a look of grief on their faces.

"I asked him to get us Mexican." I croaked.

"Don't even start to take responsibility for this. It was his choice, his job and his decision."

I wept into my hands. I knew better than to let myself have feelings for a cop.

# Chapter 52

I sat for a long time on the veranda with my bottle of bourbon remembering his soft touch, our love making, his intense eyes and his laugh.

I finally got up and headed in. I decided on a hot shower and couldn't wait to be back in my own bed. I fed my girls and headed to the bathroom. I stopped, turned back to the kitchen, and turned the lock on the door.

I took a long hot shower, put on my softest of flannel pajama's and padded to the bedroom. The girls were already on the bed, just happy to be home again. I fell into an exhausted sleep.

When I woke, I went to the freezer for ice for my eyes. They were so swollen I could hardly see out of them. I put on a pot of coffee and lowered myself into a chair.

What had happened? Was it my fault? I asked for the God dammed Mexican food! He'd be alive today if it weren't for me. How do I get through this, I thought. Just then the door bell rang. I drug myself to the door and it was Detective Christensen. He looked like shit. I invited him in and offered coffee as I had on that first morning he came to see me, again he declined.

"I just wanted to come by and see how you were doing. You don't look so good. Is there anything I can bring you?"

"No thank you, Detective. When is the funeral?"

"Friday, 10:00 a.m. I'll pick you up."

"Thanks Detective, I'd appreciate that."

"Well, I'd better go, I've got a lot of paperwork to get through."

I watched him drive slowly away, and felt an incredible emptiness engulf me. I sat and stared out the window most of the day. By 4:00 I decided I needed a drink, and mixed myself one. I needed to eat dinner tonight. I couldn't remember the last time I had eaten. Memories of asking Joe for Mexican flooded me and I started to cry. To feel that Joe gave his life for mine was overwhelming.

## Chapter 53

The funeral procession was incredible. So many police cars. Detective Christensen picked me up as promised, and he looked a little better today.

"How are you?" I asked.

"Getting by."

"You?" he asked. "I had asked Joe on a couple of occasions if there was something going on between the two of you, but he would always avoid the answer."

"Yes, Detective, there was something going on between us, but I guess I'll never know how that might have turned out."

After the funeral, and Detective Christensen dropped me off I had no idea what to do. I changed my clothes and sunk into a chair. Well, I couldn't continue to go on like this! I knew he was a cop, I said I didn't want to be involved with a cop, but I got involved with him anyway! So, pay the price! I needed to move on with my life and I'd get through this time with my work.

I did have a lot of work to do, so I heaved myself from the chair and gathered my notes. I'd call Mrs. Thoroughgood and Mrs. Jefferson to schedule appointments to go over my ideas. I picked up phone and made my calls.

Then I left messages for Ellen White and Mrs. Hawthorne to reschedule the delivery. I really was looking forward to pulling it all together, it really was going to be beautiful.

I didn't feel like working very much and decided to create something special for dinner, but first, I'd take the girls for a walk on the beach. I grabbed the leashes and we headed out.

It was a beautiful sun shiny day, and I still had all my preparations for Christmas to accomplish. I started to make a mental list.

As I came up to Jack and Michael's home, I could see them out on the veranda. They waived me up and offered me a drink, which I gladly accepted. They both hugged me and told me how glad they were that I was all right.

"Too bad for the cop." Jack snorted. "Tried to insinuate that we were into drugs!"

I didn't say anything, because I knew how thorough Joe was. We made small talk, I finished my drink and said I needed to head home.

For dinner I decided on a Porterhouse grilled medium rare, a green salad, and a garlic roll. I lit the grill and started on the salad. I had a few things that were still fresh, and I chopped red pepper, mushrooms and black olives. I found one of the Roma tomatoes that was still good, removed the brown parts from the celery and chopped some onion. I opened a bottle of wine and poured a large glass. I went to the veranda and threw the steak on the grill. By then the oven was hot and I put the garlic rolls in. I took my salad and the wine to the veranda and sat down. This reminded me so much of the night with Joe when he first made love to me.

I flipped over my steak, got the bread from the oven and started on my salad. After a few minutes I took the steak from the grill and sat back down. As I slowly ate, I remembered the times when Joe made me feel good and laugh. It's just one of those things that wasn't meant to be, I guess. But I needed to move on from this. Detective Christensen was right, I didn't need to take responsibility because Joe chose his career, and he had loved his work. He died doing what he loved to do, and that's exactly why I said I didn't want to get involved with a cop.

I sat for a long time reevaluating life, my career, and my business, and I knew I was doing what I loved to do too. Tomorrow morning I would reschedule Mrs. Hawthorn's delivery, then get on to my other new clients.

The End

# About the Author

Rosellen Price studied Interior Design and period furniture in college. She lives with her lvoing fiance and her three shih-tzu's, Topas, Onyx and their new little Emerald in the country in the Midwest. This is her first hardcover debut.

Printed in the United States
45770LVS00006B/1-24